"Perfect,

He cocked his ~~...~~
now ... I'll give y~~...~~ ~~...~~ a week."

"This is crazy," Christine muttered. But that kind of money could wipe out her debt in no time. The temptation was hard to resist. "It's nothing fancy." She felt driven to protest.

"Why don't you show me?" he suggested.

Christine hesitated, feeling awkward about letting him in. But if he didn't like it, that was his problem. She wasn't ashamed of her home or her background.

"I promise I'll be good," he said in a teasingly persuasive voice.

Christine sighed her surrender. "Why do I have the feeling that you always get your own way?"

"Because I work hard at it? Because I don't give up? Because I know what I want?"

"Maybe," said Christine dryly, "because you pay for it."

EMMA DARCY nearly became an actress until her fiancé declared he preferred to attend the theater *with* her. She became a wife and mother. Later, she took up oil painting—unsuccessfully, she remarks. Then she tried architecture, designing the family home in New South Wales. Next came romance writing—"the hardest and most challenging of all the activities," she confesses.

Books by Emma Darcy

HARLEQUIN PRESENTS

HARLEQUIN ROMANCE

EMMA DARCY

The Upstairs Lover

Harlequin Books

TORONTO • NEW YORK • LONDON
AMSTERDAM • PARIS • SYDNEY • HAMBURG
STOCKHOLM • ATHENS • TOKYO • MILAN
MADRID • WARSAW • BUDAPEST • AUCKLAND

Harlequin Presents first edition May 1993
ISBN 0-373-11555-5

THE UPSTAIRS LOVER

CHAPTER ONE

CHRISTINE had the weirdest sensation of her heart turning over.

It would have been absurd to say he was the man of her dreams. She had never conjured up an image of what the perfect man for her should look like. Yet if she were to dream . . .

He leaned indolently against one of the plane trees in the Newcombe Street Mall, where jugglers were putting on an act with flaming torches. The buskers were not holding his attention. His gaze wandered, idly surveying the crowd.

He was part of the scene but detached from it. In some curious way he did not belong. Yet Christine could not say he was out of place in such a cosmopolitan city as Sydney. The Saturday bazaar at Paddington drew people from every walk of life, and the glorious sunny day had drawn a bigger crowd than usual. With the taste of summer in the air and Christmas only six weeks away, the open-air bazaar was a popular place to be.

Tall, dark and handsome simply didn't say it all. A wistful smile played over Christine's lips as she mentally catalogued everything about him.

His thick black hair was cropped short to the long column of his neck, but a deep wave drooped rakishly across his high wide forehead, inviting feminine fingers to push it aside. The style threw his eyes into emphasis. Not that they needed any more emphasis beyond the black slashes of his brows. Haughty, commanding eyes, with a touch of arrogance that set him above and apart from others, were redeemed and made utterly compelling by the long thick lashes that half veiled the dancing light in them.

Beautifully sculptured cheekbones underlined those eyes and drew attention to his strong straight nose. His mouth was full-lipped, sensual and perfectly shaped. The clean-cut firmness of his jaw line was flawed by a slight indentation in the centre of his chin, but the flaw, if it could be called that, added provocative interest to the otherwise faultless structure of his face.

His body was equally impressive, broad-shouldered, slim-hipped, with long powerful legs that gave fascinating shape to the navy slacks he wore. The long sleeves of his blue shirt were rolled up, displaying muscular forearms, and the dark tan of his skin implied a love of the outdoors. Surfing, sailing, skiing... He had the air of assurance that went with being good at any activity he chose to take up.

A silk tie hung loosely below his unbuttoned collar. A linen jacket was slung carelessly over one shoulder. The expensive clothes he wore conveyed an image which he was seemingly scorning at the moment.

The perfect man.

Christine wondered what he would be like as a person. Vain, egotistical and self-centred, perhaps. Or would he be kind, considerate and personable? Probably the former, she thought. It had been her experience that people overendowed with God's blessing tended to have exaggerated notions of their own self-importance.

Christine dragged her eyes away. The stranger had not looked at her, and she did not want to be caught staring at him. If their eyes met it would be embarrassing.

Apart from which, she had her own private affairs to deal with. Christine went through the list of gifts she had to find. With Christmas not far off, and with little money to spare, she had to buy as cheaply as she could. The bazaar was the ideal place for bargains that didn't look like bargains.

Having lived in this community all her life, Christine knew most of the regular stall holders, and they knew her. When she was a child, this area around the church and school had been her playground while her mother worked in the hotel across the road. The inhabitants of Paddo, as it was fondly called, were of a friendly and tolerant temperament, and the character of the community was still rather Bohemian.

Art, eccentricity and a cheerful disregard of any conformity or authority had been the norm since the sixties, and most of the goods on the stalls reflected these values. The unusual, the bizarre, the wild and wonderful one-off look-at-me garments or jewellery that would draw attention and comment were all to be found here. They made exciting, interesting, different gifts that didn't cost a fortune.

"You want some cherries, Christine? Beautiful cherries."

She snapped out of her reverie to smile at Gino, who was beckoning her to his fruit barrow. The roly-poly Italian was a cheerful rogue who had looked out for her as long as Christine could remember. He was as much a personality at the bazaar as her mother had been at the hotel.

The cherries did look lush and juicy and very tempting, but this early in the season, they were outrageously expensive. Christine shook her head. "Fifteen dollars a kilo is for rich people, Gino. They're too dear for me."

He laughed and leaned forward conspiratorially. "The shops down the street are charging nineteen dollars a kilo. This is cheap." His eyes twinkled as he thumped his chest. "I . . . I am more honest."

Christine grinned at this outrageous declaration. Gino did not have the same overheads as the regular shops. "I still can't afford them, Gino, even at your ridiculously low price."

"Then take some from me." He scooped up a handful and presented them to her. "You give me your beautiful smile. I give you beautiful cherries."

Christine laughingly accepted them. "You're always spoiling me, Gino. Thank you."

"We stick together. Your mamma said look after you. I look after you."

He gave her a comradely wink before turning away to serve a customer. Christine popped one of the cherries into her mouth. She swung around and almost choked on it. She found herself virtually face to face with *the perfect man*.

He smiled at her. It was a smile that did more than cause her heart to turn over. That vital organ positively flipped. His eyes were so dark they were almost black, but sparkling with interest. Interest in *her*. "Sweet?" he asked.

Christine nodded, swiftly removing the cherry pip from her mouth.

"A lot of things look better than they taste," he said, his eyes wandering over her uplifted face with lively speculation before flicking down the long fall of her tawny gold hair to where a thick tress ended on the curved swell of her breast.

Christine wore a white cotton top with her jeans. The scooped neckline and cap sleeves were modest enough, but she was suddenly and intensely conscious of the way the material clung snugly to the lines of her body.

"Are they worth fifteen dollars a kilo?"

"Try one for yourself," she tripped out, holding up the handful of fruit. Christine could scarcely believe this was happening. Did a dream man step into reality?

"Delicate hands, dainty feet," he mused softly as he chose a plump black cherry.

Christine's heart flushed warm blood right down to her toes, which began to curl in her open-weave sandals. Her stomach felt distinctly flighty, as well.

Christine prided herself on being sensible and level-headed, but her mind was abuzz with strange excitement at this unexpected encounter.

"Beggars tend to be flatterers," she said dryly, trying for a matter-of-fact composure that would hide his extraordinary effect on her. "And flatterers are always beggars," she added for good measure.

He laughed. "If the cherries are worth the price, I'll buy you some."

"You'd be wasting your money. I don't take gifts from strangers."

"To prove I'm not a beggar. Nor a flatterer," he argued, then popped the fruit into his mouth, his eyes inviting her to wait as he tasted it. "Delicious," he declared, removing the pip and tossing it into a nearby receptacle.

"Then buy some for yourself." She gave a prompting wave towards the fruit barrow as she moved to step past him.

"Don't go," he said, a soft seductive persuasion in his voice. It was a cultured voice. An educated voice. A voice that matched his elegant, fashionable clothes.

She looked him straight in the eye. "You might not be a beggar, but you are a stranger. And I don't play with strangers."

"I want to meet you so we won't be strangers."

His directness startled her into reconsidering the situation. "Why?" she asked, still off balance at being confronted by a fantasy in the flesh.

His mouth twisted into a self-mocking little smile. "Because you're beautiful. Because you walk with a grace that makes other women look like camels in comparison. Because I want to know the colour of your eyes, see you smile, hear you talk. I looked at you and found you utterly compelling."

Christine was dumbfounded that *he* felt attracted to *her*. She privately acknowledged that the way she walked was a legacy from the ballet lessons her mother had insisted upon, with starry-eyed dreams for her daughter. But *beautiful* was certainly stretching it.

"Green eyes," he said, as though it was an enchanting surprise. "With that wonderful mane of golden hair I thought they would be a sherry brown or amber. But green is better," he murmured with satisfaction.

He was flirting outrageously with her. "I'm glad I've made your day," Christine tossed off blithely, telling herself to get her feet firmly on the ground. A man like this one didn't find what he was looking for in a woman at the Paddington Bazaar. He had to be playing some sort of game with her. Easing boredom. Filling in time.

"I'd like the chance to improve on that," he said suggestively.

Christine took a deep breath and clutched at her common sense. A stranger was still a stranger, no matter how gorgeous he looked. In fact, the more gorgeous he looked the more dangerous his motives. His extravagant compliments were definitely too flattering to take seriously. She cocked her head to one side and gave him a considering stare.

"Are you trying to pick me up?" she demanded bluntly.

"No. I don't think you're that kind of woman," he assured her. "I saw you and an impulsive madness came over me. The urge to pluck you away from this crowd and take you somewhere quiet with me where we could talk..."

"You expected me to say yes?" Christine laughed at him, enjoying his bold and outrageous charm, but letting him know she was not fatuously taken in by it.

His answering grin was loaded with mischievous appeal. "I'd hoped that you would say yes."

He certainly had a healthy ego, Christine thought, but he was very personable with it. With his looks and charm, he was probably used to getting any woman he fancied. All she could be to a man like him was a passing fancy. A surge of pride stubbornly squashed the temptation he offered.

"The answer is no."

"My name is Shane," he persisted.

"I have things to do," Christine stated on an emphatically purposeful note.

"Any reason we can't do them together?" he asked, unperturbed by her rejection of his approach.

"They're personal."

"And if I want to see you again?"

She threw him a mocking little smile. "If you're so madly interested in me, you'll have to find me."

His mouth quirked in wry appreciation of her challenge. "I presume I'm not allowed to follow you."

"If you do, I'll get one of my friends to call a policeman," she warned, waving her hand to indicate the stall holders.

"So this is goodbye?" He did not look the least bit chastened by her decision. His eyes were dancing with teasing amusement.

Christine reacted with haughty dignity. "Yes. This is goodbye."

As she turned away, he was audacious enough to blow a kiss after her. Her whole body burned with awareness of his watching eyes as she pushed through the crowd, blindly seeking to put a block of people between her and stupid temptation.

Physical attraction had a way of clouding one's judgement. Christine had learned that lesson recently enough to be wary of giving in to it again, particularly with a man who was clearly beyond her league. It didn't work. It never would work. Dreams had to be recognised as dreams, and not confused with the social realities of life. It would be the ultimate stupidity to think for one moment something good might have developed if she'd agreed to go along with *him*.

A pick-up. That was how he would have thought of her. As it was, she had supplied him with an easy diversion. Had he noticed her staring at him beforehand? She hadn't thought so, but the idea made her squirm with embarrassment until she reminded herself she had decisively refuted any implication that she had been signalling a come-on.

She looked back but he had not followed her. Without active pursuit, there was simply no way he could possibly find her in a city of four million people. At least, she thought, brightening, some good had come of the encounter. The stranger named Shane was buying cherries from Gino. Gino would be pleased.

CHAPTER TWO

CHRISTINE stepped off the hot sidewalk and under the shade of the trees. The cluster of native eucalypts had been planted by the council when it was decided to turn her narrow little lane into a cul-de-sac, shutting off the busy traffic of Oxford Street. She glanced back one last time but saw no-one who resembled the perfect man.

She shrugged away a perverse feeling of disappointment. Her warning had definitely put him off. Besides, why would a perfect man follow a woman who had proved hard to get? More than likely he was used to women following him, or at least collapsing into a compliant heap if he showed interest in them.

His interest in her had only been fleeting. There was nothing to regret. He did not belong to her world. Christine knew from painful personal experience that getting out of one's league could lead to devastating disillusionment. Better for her that he hadn't tried to pursue her.

She looked up at the old terrace house her mother had been so proud of owning. It was the standard two rooms up and two rooms down, with an annexe at the back for the utility rooms. No garden, no swimming pool, only basic working-class living quarters, the same

as all the others in the row. But to Rose Delaney, it had
represented a proper home for herself and her daughter, the kind of security no-one could take away.

Of the whole terrace row, it definitely looked the best
cared for. The old bricks had been blasted clean of a
century of grime, the intricately patterned wrought-
iron railing on the narrow verandas painted forest
green, and a tiled roof had replaced the sagging slate.

Her mother had been delighted with the renovations. Neither of them had foreseen Christine would be
left alone to pay off the mortgage that had made them
possible. But then, even the doctor Christine had called
in when her mother had been so ill with influenza had
not foreseen the sudden onset of viral pneumonia.

It had been hard to accept that her mother, who had
always been so brightly alive, could die with such unexpected swiftness. It had made Christine feel her
nursing experience futile, and her grief had been
haunted with wondering if she could have done something more, something different. But nothing she
thought or felt could bring her mother back. Life went
on, forcing Christine to face its problems.

She heaved a deep sigh as she juggled her shopping
bags so she could open the front gate. Perhaps it was
stupid to keep struggling to make ends meet. If she put
the house on the market, she would have money
enough to pay off the mortgage and a tidy sum to in-
vest, as well. That was the commonsense solution. Yet
she could not bring herself to take it. It felt too much
like a betrayal.

What she needed right now was a prompt response to the advertisement she had put in this morning's newspaper. If she didn't let the two upstairs rooms soon she would be in financial difficulties again. Her nurse's pay only went so far. After living expenses, she could barely make the interest payments on the loan from the bank. Reducing the debt was beyond her personal income.

Christine glanced at her watch as she dumped her bags on the porch to fish the door key out of her pocket. She had stipulated after two o'clock for callers. There was an hour left for her to put her shopping away, wrap the Christmas gifts she had bought and do a final tidy up.

The house felt depressingly empty. Christine moved quickly down the hallway, hoping that whoever turned up would be as congenial as Sandra Allsop, with whom she had shared the house for the past six months. Sandra had rented both upstairs rooms, using one as a workplace for her restoration of paintings. A big assignment had taken her to Melbourne, and while Christine wished Sandra well in her career, she really missed her bright company.

When the doorbell rang at five minutes to two, her spirits lifted. Someone was eager to look at the rooms. Willing it to be a person she could like, Christine pasted a welcoming smile on her face and opened the door.

The perfect man was standing on her porch.

He was even more perfectly presented with his jacket on, his collar buttoned and his tie in place.

Christine's smile dropped into a gape as her heart performed a double loop. Her mind went into a dizzy spin, whirling around the plain, unmistakable fact: he had taken up her challenge and found her. The dark eyes danced with teasing triumph.

"Hello again," he said, his mouth breaking into a dazzling grin.

"How...?" The word was barely a croak. She closed her mouth and swallowed hard. The insides of her body were misbehaving in a most disorderly fashion. She managed better at the second attempt at coherency. "How did you get here? Find me?"

"After much haggling over my intentions, your friend Gino was finally persuaded into giving me your name and address."

Christine rolled her eyes at this indiscretion. "How many kilos of cherries did you end up buying?"

"Two."

"Sold for thirty pieces of silver," Christine concluded with a rueful sigh.

"Not at all. Dark and dire threats hang over my head if you report to Gino that he did wrong. I had to swear by everything I hold dear that you'd invited me to find you."

"I did not!"

"Yes, you did," he corrected laughingly. "If I was so madly interested, I could find you. That's what you said. And that's what I've done. So we're not strangers anymore."

Christine shook her head dazedly. "I still don't know you."

"That can be very easily fixed. I couldn't get Gino to leave his barrow until the bazaar ends at four o'clock, but he agreed I could use him as a proxy for an introduction, so if you'll pretend he's here..."

He stepped to one side and waved to the space he had left. "Christine, I would like you to meet Shane Courtney, a man of impeccable character, single, unattached, in respectable employment and wanting very much to know you."

Then he waved from the space to her. "Shane, I would like you to meet Christine Delaney, a woman of prudence and sensibility, single, unattached, a true disciple of Florence Nightingale, whose rare beauty is undoubtedly a tonic to all the patients she looks after."

He stepped back to face her and offered his hand. "How do you do, Miss Delaney? Or may I have the pleasure of calling you Christine?"

All her defences crumbled under the irresistible appeal of his charm and persistence. She took his hand, laughing at the formality of his introduction. "I'll have to concede you've won that privilege, Shane."

"Thank you." His hand curled warmly around hers, making her skin tingle with excitement. The dark eyes sparkled with delight as he lifted the bulging bag in his other hand. "I need you to help me eat all these cherries. And to assure you I'm totally harmless, we could stroll to a public park where you can tell me the story of your life."

"I'm sorry." She truly was. "But I can't today."

"Why not? Haven't I carried out the quest? Fulfilled your requirements? Shown myself a true knight of the realm? Won some favour with the fair lady?" His eyebrows waggled in appeal.

Christine couldn't help laughing, and her disappointment at having to let him down was acute. "For such gallantry, I'd present you with my handkerchief if I had one, but the truth is I have to stay in. I've advertised rooms to let and..."

"Just what I want. I'll take them."

"You?" Christine was jolted into withdrawing her hand from his seductive grasp.

"Sure! This position is very handy for me, and I'm sick of staying in hotels. As a matter of fact, I was looking for an apartment to rent in this area, but there was nothing suitable listed at the estate agents'."

So that was what he had been doing in Paddington this morning, Christine thought. The bazaar had simply been a place to pause, not to browse. "Look, uh, Shane... It's not a separate apartment. Only two rooms and a bathroom upstairs. The kitchen is downstairs, which you'd have to share with me. And—"

"Perfect!"

"—*and* I advertised for a young woman. Not by any stretch of the imagination do you fit that description."

He lowered his brows. "Is this a case of sexual discrimination, Christine?"

She took a deep breath. "It's my house and I can choose whomever I want to share it with," she declared evenly.

He cocked his head to one side. "Let's see now," he mused. "I'm paying over two hundred dollars a night for my hotel room. If I paid you a thousand dollars a week for the upstairs rooms and a share of your kitchen, would that do away with the objection that I'm not a woman?"

A thousand!

Christine had figured on charging a weekly rate of seventy-five dollars a room, which was very reasonable in the high-rental climate of Sydney. An extra eight hundred and fifty dollars would wipe out her debt in no time. Yet in all honesty, how could she accept it?

"This is crazy," she muttered, shaking her head over the unrealistic offer.

"Not to me, it isn't," he insisted. "I'll not only save money, I'll also have you to talk to when we pass in the kitchen. Won't be so lonely as being by myself."

"But... it's nothing fancy," Christine felt driven to protest. The temptation of all that money was hard to resist. If he didn't mind paying it, if he was paying out that kind of money anyway, it wasn't wrong for her to accept it, was it?

"Why don't you show me?" he suggested reasonably.

Christine hesitated, feeling awkward about letting him into the house. He would soon see. But if he didn't like the house that was his problem, not hers. She was not ashamed of her home or her background, and it was just as well to establish the ground between them before committing herself to any further involvement with him.

"I promise I'll be good," he said in a teasingly persuasive voice.

Christine sighed her surrender. "Why do I get the feeling that you always get your own way?"

"Because I work hard at it? Because I don't give up? Because I know what I want?"

"Or maybe because you pay for it," Christine said dryly.

His mouth twisted in wry acknowledgement. "Sometimes money helps. But it doesn't buy all you want."

"Good point," Christine agreed. "Keep remembering it. I wouldn't like you to think that this landlady's favours come with the territory."

He grinned at the none-too-subtle warning. "Do I get to come in now?"

"I'll show you the rooms. Then if you still want them I'll consider your offer," Christine stated cautiously, but her heart was drumming a wild tattoo as she stood back to wave him inside.

The moment she shut the door behind him, she was acutely conscious of the narrowness of the hallway and his filling it with overpowering masculinity. Christine was not a small woman. She was above average height and generously curved. She was also quite strong from all the lifting she did in her work at the hospital. But somehow Shane Courtney reduced her to weak, quivering femininity. It took all her willpower to lead off down the hallway like a landlady in command of her domain.

"What's in there?" he asked as they passed the first door.

"*My* room. Which is private and personal," Christine emphasised.

"Naturally," he murmured, a lilt of amusement in his voice.

Christine felt her stomach tighten. Could she trust him to respect her privacy? Could she trust herself not to succumb to the temptation of knowing all the realities he might pursue with her? On the other hand, it could be an experience worth having.

As that last thought slid into her mind, Christine gave herself a severe mental shake. It wasn't her natural turn of thought at all. Casual sex was simply not her scene. It didn't have good results. Apart from which, it was downright dangerous these days. Having the perfect man turn up on her doorstep clearly made impulsive madness infectious.

The hallway opened into the living room, which gave her some breathing space from the close physical awareness that was causing havoc with her system. "You can eat your meals here. Watch TV if you like," she said quickly, skirting the table and chairs and indicating the well-worn but comfortable armchairs grouped for viewing the old-fashioned box television in the corner.

Everything was old and well-worn. The oak dining table and chairs, the big sideboard, the floral carpet her mother had loved, the lace curtains at the window. Shane Courtney was probably thinking he had stepped back fifty years, except for the TV, which was only fifteen years old. But everything was clean and well cared for, Christine reminded herself with stubborn pride.

She waved to the narrow staircase that hugged one wall. "As you can see, there's no private entrance for you. You have to come through here."

"No problem," he said.

Christine strode quickly to the renovated annexe. Plain tiles, synthetic surfaces, all white except for the beige linoleum floor. It was not, by any means, a fancy kitchen, but it gave a sense of light and definitely looked clean and hygienic.

"You get half the space in the fridge and the pantry cupboard for your food supplies," Christine rattled out. "I'll show you how to use the stove and anything else you'll need to know. You're expected to wash your own dishes after meals and put everything back the way you found it."

She didn't look to see how he reacted to that, moving straight onto the laundry to point out the small automatic washer and dryer and the ironing facilities.

"What's through that door?" he asked, when she was about to usher him out.

"*My* shower and toilet."

"Right. Off-limits?"

"Yes. There's a bathroom upstairs for your use."

He gave her a smile that seemed to express both satisfaction and approval. It was a smile that curled around Christine's heart and squeezed it, making her forget what she was supposed to be doing for several moments.

Apparently he was not the least put off by what he had seen so far. Nor by the prospect of having to clean up after himself. "There are only the upstairs rooms to look at now," Christine said, needing him to unblock the passage to the kitchen.

He obligingly moved and Christine found it easier to breathe. "Mind if I leave these here?" he asked, lifting the bag of cherries onto the kitchen sink.

"That's okay. Please go on up and look for yourself. You'll feel more free to check out the rooms if I don't come with you," she said in a rush, far too conscious of his physical effect on her to accompany him into bedrooms.

"As you wish," he said easily, but his eyes held a knowing gleam that showed he was well aware of her awareness of him as a man. And of herself as a woman. And the attraction between them, shimmering like live electricity.

Christine stayed in the kitchen, her body tensed as she listened to the creak of his footfalls on the old treads of the staircase. Not until he had stepped off the top landing did she move. Then she whirled into the small bathroom at the back of the laundry and stared at her face in the mirror.

Did he really think her beautiful? Christine examined her reflection critically, trying to see what he saw. A mane of golden hair, he had said. Certainly an exaggeration—the mass of her hair was darker than gold. Sandra had talked her into a few artistic lighter streaks through the feathery fringe and various long strands on either side of her face. They were gold.

The fine arch of her brow was brown, as were her lashes, and they highlighted her green eyes, but Christine didn't consider her eyes startling in any way. They were not a vivid sparkly green, more like the green of still rock pools.

Her nose was neat enough, straight but ending in a slight flare at the nostrils. This did seem to balance her rather generous mouth. She felt her face was too strongly boned for real beauty, yet the overall effect was individual and attractive, particularly when she smiled. People did tend to look at her when she smiled. Her teeth were very good, white and straight and even. Christine was justly proud of her teeth.

Sandra had suggested she had the kind of distinctive looks that made a good model, but Christine wasn't interested in that kind of life. She had always wanted to be a nurse and she found the job very rewarding. It had to be, because a nurse's salary was hardly rewarding. In Christine's opinion nurses were grossly underpaid for the work they did.

Which brought her back to money.

Whether Shane Courtney thought her beautiful or not was not the point she should be considering. This was a financial situation, not a social one. Although clearly he meant it to be social, as well. The critical question, on both counts, was how long did he mean it to go on?

Christine moved to the kitchen and worked on a sensible composure while she waited for him. When she heard the creak of the stairs she went into the living room to meet him. Perhaps the lack of modern luxury upstairs had changed his mind about staying.

Christine saw a look of grim satisfaction on his face as he turned to take the last two steps to the living room. Then he caught sight of her, and for a moment a fierce blaze of purpose shone from his eyes, encompassing her in a way that was far from flirtatious.

Perhaps she had been blinded by his looks and charm, but Christine was instantly jolted out of any impression that Shane Courtney was a playboy. He might have plenty of money to splash around, but there was relentless steel behind his handsome facade, and an arrogance of mind that went deeper than self-assurance.

He suddenly looked more mature, more authoritative. Christine assessed his age at thirty or more, which meant he was at least six years older than she was, and there could be no doubt that his experience of life was far wider. Whatever game he had embarked on, Christine sensed he was utterly determined to carry it through.

His face relaxed into a reassuringly friendly smile as he crossed the room and held out a cheque, already written out for a thousand dollars. "My first week's rent. Is it okay for me to move in tomorrow morning?"

Christine took the slip of paper and stared at it, wildly wondering if she might be selling her soul to the devil. She had a premonition that her life was to be irrevocably changed by Shane Courtney's coming. She looked up, trying to divine his intentions in his eyes, but all she saw was a warm admiration that increased her pulse.

"How long do you intend to stay here?" she asked.

"That depends."

"On what?"

"Many things."

Her, for one, was the unspoken but unmistakeable message in his eyes. Christine forced herself to ignore it. "That rather leaves me in the dark, Shane. If it's only for a week, I could tell anyone who comes this afternoon that I'll have vacant rooms again by next weekend."

He shook his head. "Don't do that, Christine. I promise you won't lose financially by my staying here."

"Where do you normally live?"

He shrugged. "Wherever my work takes me."

"It's brought you here?"

"No. My grandfather had a heart attack a few days ago. He's in St. Vincent's Hospital and may be there for some time having tests done. I don't know how long. I don't know what I'll be doing when he's released from hospital, either. It depends . . . on a lot of things."

Courtney. Max Courtney in the vascular unit, who had jokingly called the visits by his family the gathering of the vultures, waiting for him to die. Christine felt herself go cold. She liked the eccentric old tyrant, but his sons and their wives had made her bristle with intense dislike. She had met their kind before, and it had been a bitter unforgettable experience.

And this was the son of those people.

The son and heir.

Christine knew now precisely where she was with Shane Courtney. She folded the cheque and put it in her jeans pocket, no longer feeling the least bit guilty about taking so much money from him. It gave her a great deal of satisfaction.

She gave him a bright plastic smile. "I understand. If you pay me the same amount at the beginning of each week, you're welcome to stay here as long as you like." Then in a few quick strides, she retrieved the bag of cherries from the kitchen and thrust it into his hands. "You should take these to your grandfather when you visit him. They'll be a nice treat for him."

His laugh was a bark of heavy irony. "You don't know my grandfather."

"I know that patients like a change from hospital food," she replied, deciding there was no reason to enlighten him as to her knowledge of Max Courtney. She swung around and headed for the hallway. "Tomorrow morning will be fine for moving in. I'll give you a key to the front door when you get here."

He had little choice but to follow her out. Christine opened the door for him and stood aside, pointedly waiting for him to go. He paused beside her, a slight frown of puzzlement on his brow. The dark eyes probed hers intently, searching for what had changed, but Christine returned a cool serene look that denied him entry to her thoughts and feelings.

His mouth curled into a teasing little smile as he murmured, "Tomorrow is another day. I'll be here at eleven o'clock, Christine."

"Fine."

"I'd like to take you out to lunch."

"Do I get to choose the place?"

"Wherever you want."

Her smile held much hidden satisfaction. "Thank you. I'd like that, Shane."

He rested content and went.

Christine closed the door on him and felt content, too, a savage kind of content. She knew precisely where she would take Shane Courtney for lunch tomorrow. She was going to lay it all out for him so he knew where he was with her.

She patted her jeans pocket as she went into her room. The money was hers, however he reacted tomorrow. And serve him right for thinking he could use her as he willed!

CHAPTER THREE

SHANE COURTNEY arrived promptly at eleven o'clock the next morning. He brought with him a leather suitcase, a black plastic suitbag, a hard vinyl briefcase and an air of pleasurable anticipation. He wore a many-pocketed, pin-tucked green sports shirt that screamed exclusive boutique-wear for men, and white jeans that fitted like a glove, leaving no doubt about the manliness of his physique.

One thing could certainly be said of Shane Courtney. He was not hiding his light under a bushel. He emitted a flesh-and-blood vibrancy that almost destroyed Christine's resolutions. She wished he wasn't quite so devastatingly handsome.

The way he looked at her didn't help, either. He took in her appearance with a hungry possessiveness, dismissing her off-the-peg outfit as totally irrelevant. She might as well not have clothes on at all, Christine thought, feeling her skin prickle with heat.

She had rebelliously chosen the off-the-shoulder black stretchy top and her pleated mustard miniskirt to show him what he was *not* going to get, but the idea was backfiring on her with a vengeance. She felt intensely vulnerable as his gaze skated down the long shapeliness of her bare legs.

"Good morning," she said to make him concentrate on proper formalities.

"Very good," he replied, his eyes dancing to hers with compelling brilliance. "Never been better. I think I've been living all my life to reach this moment."

"Well, now that moment has passed," Christine advised him with truly wonderful aplomb. "Who knows what surprises there'll be in the future?"

For him especially, she silently promised herself. She was not, absolutely not, going to succumb to his superficial charm.

She stood back and waved him inside. "Go on up," she invited. "Everything's ready for you. I left a key to the front door on the dressing-table in the back room."

"Thank you." He moved straight past her, not waiting to be shown the way. "I'll take my things upstairs and be down immediately."

"Don't hurry. It's only eleven, and I have things to do. If we leave for lunch at twelve-thirty, that will suit me fine."

He paused at the end of the hallway to look at her, one eyebrow cocked in appeal. "Can I help in any way?"

"My business is still the same as yesterday. *Private.*"

Christine had, in fact, done all her weekend chores. She was simply letting Shane Courtney know that he couldn't take it for granted her time was his whenever he liked.

He bestowed his dazzling smile on her. "Isn't there any other option? Waiting so long will seem like another lifetime."

"I'm sure it won't be that bad," Christine said somewhat acidly. "Undoubtedly a man of your intelligence will find something to occupy his time."

"Foiled!" he said, and his smile grew broader, as though he could read her like a book and knew exactly what she was up to. "But I do make a good handyman," he continued, "if there are some odd little jobs you would like done. Perhaps that would divert my thoughts away from you."

Christine laughed at the image of Shane Courtney being a general handyman around a house. "I'll keep it in mind," she warned. "But at the moment, there are no little jobs to do."

He heaved an exaggerated sigh. "Then I shall have to possess my soul with patience."

"Do that," she tossed at him, then went into her room, shutting him out.

She picked up the library book she had been reading, settled herself on the sofa by the window and opened it at the bookmark. Her mind kept wandering from the words on the page and she soon gave up trying to concentrate on the story. Shane Courtney was right. An hour and a half was going to be a devilishly long time.

Floorboards creaked overhead, indicating that he had chosen to sleep in the room above hers. That was a disturbing thought. It wasn't the same as when Sandra had occupied that bedroom.

It was only for a week or two, Christine reasoned. Surely Shane Courtney wouldn't stay longer than that. Not at the ridiculous price he was paying. The money was worth a bit of disturbance. To diminish the debt would be marvellous.

Once she had paid off the mortgage, she would continue to let rooms for a while, build up some savings, then perhaps gradually refurnish the house to her own taste.

The room she was in had been the parlour while her mother was alive, a far cry from the bed-sit Christine had organised for herself in order to make the upstairs rooms available for letting. She imagined how it could be, given a sense of freedom to buy whatever she liked. It would be lovely to turn the house into a proper home again.

On the other hand, it would be lonely living here by herself. Christine remembered the dreadful month after her mother died, feeling totally bereft, aching for all that could never be again. When Sandra had come to live upstairs, her presence had made a lot of difference. It hadn't been nearly so hard to come home from work because the house wasn't so hauntingly empty anymore.

She still missed her mother, terribly at times. The thought of Christmas by herself was a miserable ache.

Her mother's faithful old friends would press invitations to their homes for Christmas day, and they would mean kindly, but it would feel wrong for her. She would have to think of something else to do.

A few ideas slid through her mind but none of them stirred any enthusiasm. When the knock came on her door at twelve-thirty, she was startled to realise she had been daydreaming so long. Her pulse quickened at the thought of facing Shane Courtney again. Her mind insisted she deal with him as planned.

She picked up her black handbag, checked her appearance and made herself stroll casually to the door.

Christine believed in being punctual, but she was not about to fall over herself for Shane Courtney. It was irritating to find herself feeling distinctly weak-kneed when she opened the door and came face to face with him. Was the physical impact of the man ever going to lessen for her?

"Ready to go?" she asked with forced unconcern.

"*Waiting* to go," he replied, anticipation sparkling in his eyes.

"Then let's be on our way."

She was intensely conscious of him at her side as she let them both out of the house and locked up.

"Where are we off to?" he asked, his voice tinged with amused curiosity.

"Oh, up the road a bit. It's no great walk." She gave him a reassuring smile as he opened the gate for her.

"Have you lived in Paddington all your life, Christine?"

"All that I can remember of it. What about you? Where's your home?"

He shrugged as he fell into step beside her. "Wherever I happen to be."

"Because of your job?"

"Yes."

Christine shot him a curious look. "So how are you gainfully employed?"

A sardonic little smile played over his lips. "I guess you could say I'm a problem solver, when other people can't solve them for themselves. I give rocky business companies the chance at a new lease on life."

Definitely not a playboy! Christine remembered the flash of steel she had seen yesterday. The kind of problems he took on in his line of work probably indicated a ruthless type of personality. How ruthless did Shane intend to be in getting his own way with her?

A little shiver of apprehension ran down Christine's spine as she took the pathway under the trees to the main thoroughfare. Did the devil come in the form of perfection? Shane Courtney certainly knew the art of temptation. But that didn't mean she had to fall victim to it, even though she had been financially seduced into letting him invade her home.

Which reminded her that he had neatly avoided the home question, apparently not wanting to divulge information on his background. Her lips tightened with determination as she turned into Oxford Street towards her destination. She was not about to let him off the hook so easily. She tried another tack.

"Where does your grandfather live?"

There was a slight pause before he answered, as though he was reluctant to pursue the topic. Which accorded with his carefree intentions towards her, Christine thought cynically. He clearly preferred the image of a self-made man whose family was irrelevant. Which, of course, was not the truth. His kind of family was always relevant.

"He lives on the central coast, north of Sydney." The brief reply was delivered in a sardonic tone.

Christine frowned, not quite sure how to interpret that. "Did your grandfather enjoy the cherries?" she asked.

"I gave them to the nursing staff to help sweeten the trial of looking after him," Shane said, then looked amused at the shock his words provoked.

"Wasn't that a mean and pointed insult?"

He laughed outright. "Everyone connected to my grandfather calls him the General behind his back. With good reason. He's probably already started reorganising the hospital system to suit himself. I assure you, he's so self-contained he would view a gift of cherries with contempt. He would certainly consider it a sign of weakness in me."

Christine reconsidered the man beside her. It was an astute reading of the situation. As Max Courtney scornfully put it, the members of his family were currying favour. The moment they were gone, he took immense pleasure in dispatching their gifts to other patients. He had brightened up the whole ward with his behaviour. Although he did bend the system a little, he did it with such disarming panache...

Panache!

Sometimes genes skipped a generation. Max Courtney was seventy-five years of age, but he was still a handsome man and extremely clever at obtaining his own way. It would be interesting to see Shane and his grandfather together.

"Your turn," Shane said teasingly.

"For what?" Christine swiftly collected her wits. It should be irrelevant to her how Shane hit it off with his grandfather. After a week or so, they would have no place in her future.

"To tell me about yourself."

"There's not much of interest," Christine demurred, holding out for the most telling moment of truth. "What there is you'll soon learn. We're almost at the starting point."

He glanced down the street ahead, looking for a likely restaurant, then realised they were almost opposite the mall where he'd met her yesterday. He turned a laughing smile at her. "Did your life begin at the bazaar?"

"No. Here is the place where I want to have lunch," she said, pointing to a blackboard propped outside the hotel. On it was chalked the menu for the bar counter.

"Here?" It was his turn to look shocked.

"Good food at reasonable prices," Christine declared with relish, stepping up to the entrance. There was the usual boisterous Sunday crowd inside, and the smell of beer was strong.

"Christine." Shane's hand closed around her arm, halting her. He spoke with urgent persuasion. "Can't we go somewhere quieter? Price is no object. We could go—"

"You said I could choose," she reminded him, smiling away any argument.

"But…" He frowned, not wanting to offend her yet clearly repelled by her choice.

"Welcome to my world, Shane," Christine tossed at him as she moved forward, drawing him after her since he did not release her arm.

The place was packed. Every one of the stools was occupied around the bar, along the wall benches, around the chest-high drink tables that circled the floor-to-ceiling poles. There was barely standing room. It took some manoeuvring to make any headway through the crush of people.

"Hi, Christine!" Nancy called from behind the bar.

"Hey, Christine! Got yourself a follower today," one of the regular customers chirped with a knowing wink.

"Better watch out, Christine," another advised jokingly. "He doesn't look like a local."

"But he's sporting the right colour for Kitty O'Shea's Hotel," another piped up. "The green of the Irish."

"That's a fact," declared another. "We'll let him pass. Rose would have liked the looks of him."

"Rose always liked a good-looker."

"Nah! Rose liked everybody. Big-hearted woman, Rose."

"Yea to that! Good on you, Christine!" Glasses were lifted to her in a general toast. "Keep him in tow. But if he puts one finger out of line, you can count on us to rough him up."

This was followed by general laughter.

She laughed and waved at all of them as she passed, accepting their rough humour as natural and affectionate. How Shane was taking it she didn't know or care, but his grip on her arm did not slacken until she reached the staircase on the far side of the bar.

"The restaurant is upstairs," she enlightened him, glancing pointedly at the hand restraining her from moving ahead. The passageway was too narrow for two people to mount the stairs side by side.

"I see," he murmured. One eyebrow lifted in amused inquiry. "Another gauntlet for me to run?"

"It's always interesting to test a man's mettle," Christine said blithely, starting up the stairs as soon as he let her go.

Shane followed without comment.

He had certainly recovered fast from his initial distaste, Christine thought. Despite her prejudice against his social class, she was impressed by his good-humoured response to the razzing downstairs. Or perhaps he was simply quick to accept the inevitable.

Once they stepped onto the upper floor, much of the noise was left behind and there was an immediate sense of pleasant spaciousness. A wall had been knocked out to create a large room, and the hotel was of an age where the ceilings were wonderfully high. The tables in the restaurant were set well apart from each other. They were dressed with starched linen tableclothes and serviettes and with little vases of fresh flowers. To Christine's eye, the room had an old-world style and elegance that few fashionable restaurants could match.

The bar that dominated one wall was a showpiece of the past, a solid structure of polished wood with brass fittings, stained glass panels and a huge mirror along the back. Photographs of scenes from the old days were framed and hung around the walls, along with posters of films that had been huge box-office successes in their heyday. *Around the World in Eighty Days. The Prisoner of Zenda. The Lady Takes a Flyer.*

Her mother's best friend came hurrying from behind the bar the moment she saw Christine. "Lovely to see you, dear," she said, smiling a warm welcome. "Got company for lunch, have you?" She eyed Shane with heightened interest. "Table for two by the window?"

"Yes, please, Moira."

She fussed over them like a mother hen, seeing them seated, taking an order for drinks, bringing them menus, all the time taking note of everything about Shane Courtney. He bore it surprisingly well, exerting his charm on Moira until she left them alone, satisfied Christine was with a gentleman.

"Is there a Paddington mafia looking after you?" he whispered over his menu, slanting his eyebrows in mock alarm. "Will Gino suddenly appear and stand over me?"

Christine laughed and shook her head. "You're safe now. For better or for worse, you've been approved until further notice."

"Passed the test," he said with satisfaction.

"Perhaps," Christine said non-committally, and studied her menu, keeping a bland expression to block out the scrutiny she felt coming from Shane Courtney.

Jodie, one of the weekend waitresses, came with their drinks and took their order for lunch. She used the opportunity to ogle Shane, too, and gave Christine a thumbs-up sign behind his back when she left them.

Christine relaxed on the padded banquette that ran along the wall, rested her arm on the windowsill and gazed out on the tranquil scene of sunlight playing through the lovely leafy trees around the old sand-stone church. The peace of Sunday reigned in the deserted grounds.

"Pleasant view," Shane remarked.

"I was brought up mostly at this hotel," Christine said flatly. "That was my playground out there. And my school."

"So that's why everyone knows you," he said quietly.

"And looks out for me." She turned to him with a wistful reminiscent smile. "My mother used to ask everyone to look out for me. She ran the bar downstairs for almost twenty years, and before that she was a live-in maid here. The owners were kind enough to take her into their employment and give her a chance."

"Rose."

He gave her mother's name a soft respect that brought a film of tears to Christine's eyes. She quickly turned her head to the window again. A warm hand covered hers, fingers stroking a silent comfort that Christine wasn't sure she wanted from him. His touch made her feel more agitated than soothed.

"Was there a problem?" he asked sympathetically.

It stirred a tumult of defensive pride. She swung around to face him, her green eyes blazing a fierce challenge. "Yes," she snapped. "The problem was me. My mother wanted to keep me. But she had nowhere to go and no-one to turn to. You see, Mr. Courtney, illegitimate babies weren't so acceptable in those days, and neither were their mothers. They're still not in some circles."

She paused, then savagely rammed the point home. "Being the bastard daughter of a barmaid tends to make me less beautiful, don't you think, Mr. Courtney? Maybe still desirable enough for a little intimate dalliance, but the buck *will* stop there, *won't* it?"

CHAPTER FOUR

SHANE COURTNEY was not the least bit taken aback by
Christine's blistering assertions. Far from recoiling
from her, he leaned forward and enclosed her hand in
both of his.

"So that's why you have a hostile and defensive in-
feriority complex," he said in a low and caring voice.

It swept the ground out from under Christine's feet.
It propelled her into an outraged denial of what felt like
an attack on her.

"I am not hostile," she snapped.

"I am not defensive," she squawked.

Then with firmer control over her voice, she hotly
insisted, "And most certainly I do not have an inferi-
ority complex! I'm as good as anyone!"

"Christine . . . I'm on your side," he said with persuasive gentleness. "I can help you."

She snatched her hand out of his and nursed it on her
lap, rubbing at it with the fingers of her other hand to
take away the blood-tingling heat he had pressed upon
it. "I don't need help, thank you," she bit out, glaring
her rejection of all the implications in such a suggestion.

He spread his hands open in appeal. "I didn't mean you can't hold your own, Christine. You more than do that." A whimsical little smile teased for a truce. "And I admire and respect you for it."

"Do you indeed?" she queried sceptically.

"Yes. Very much." He relaxed in his chair, smoothly easing the tension between them. "And I admire your mother for keeping you in what must have been extremely difficult circumstances," he added with what sounded like genuine sincerity.

Christine stared at him, watching for any shift of expression that might belie what he was projecting, but the dark eyes returned her scrutiny unflinchingly and his face remained completely serious.

"It was the biggest decision of her life," Christine said flatly. "It wasn't easy for her to find employment to support herself and a baby."

"Couldn't her family help her?"

"Her father disowned her when he found out she was pregnant. He was a church warden," Christine said. with bitter irony. "A widower. And she was his only child, who had been his cook and housekeeper most of her young life. She was only eighteen, completely untrained for any career, but he banished her from his home and told her he never wanted to see her again."

"A hard man," Shane murmured.

"And a bigoted one. But in the end he did help her," she said with the satisfaction of justice having been finally done. "He died and left enough money for my mother to buy the terrace house. So she got a home for both of us after all."

"Do you know who your father was, Christine?"

She gave a rueful grimace. "Yes. His name was Chris Lanigan. My mother told me he was beautiful and funny and she loved him. She always said I look just like him."

"Why didn't he stand by her? Marry her?"

"He was a construction worker. He was crushed to death with many others when the fifth floor of the Merrick building collapsed. My mother lost him before she even knew she was pregnant. So she was left to fend for herself."

"She didn't try to contact his family...about you?"

Christine shook her head sadly. "They didn't want to know. They had seven other children and they didn't want to take responsibility for the wild oats sown by their dead son. They called my mother a bad girl, and it wasn't in my mother's nature to impose herself where she wasn't wanted."

"I'm sorry."

"Are you really?"

"To be so totally abandoned by those who should have cared..." He winced. "It shouldn't happen to anyone."

The deep ring of sympathetic concern in his voice carried conviction. Christine found it more and more difficult to hold on to her prejudice against him.

"How long did it take for your mother to find her way to this hotel?" he asked.

"That was later," Christine told him. "She went to a home for wayward girls where she could stay to have her baby. She was pressed to give me up for adoption, but she wouldn't do it. I was a very much loved child."

He nodded. "Did your mother have any idea of the hardship it would create for herself?"

"She was determined to manage somehow. And when she was finally accepted here, she really landed on her feet. Everyone was so kind, helping to keep an eye on me while she worked. Once I was a toddler, some of the regular customers would take me out for a walk, buy me lollies and ice-cream. I had a lot of honorary uncles and aunties when I was a kid." She smiled. "Still have."

"Your mother entrusted you to some of those men downstairs?"

The slightly critical note instantly wiped out Christine's smile. "Rough exteriors don't mean that people don't have good hearts, Shane Courtney." Her green eyes flashed sharp animosity. "It's my experience that the more smoothly sophisticated people become, the meaner hearts they hold."

His mouth twisted with wry appreciation of her observation. "You're right." His eyes locked onto hers, and Christine had the confusing sensation of sharing an insight that he recognised only too well. "I agree. The smoother they get, the meaner they are," he repeated grimly.

Jodie broke into the moment, setting their starters on the table and inviting them to enjoy the beautifully presented food. Christine stared at her king prawns, coated with a coconut sauce and accompanied with slices of mango. She wondered if she had badly misjudged Shane Courtney. What experience had he lived through to make him agree with her? Then she shrugged off the question and began eating. Time would tell if she was right or wrong about him.

"Great oysters," Shane remarked, attacking the Sydney rock oysters he had ordered with relish.

"I told you the food was good," she said, nodding to the other tables, which were now mostly taken.

He grinned at her. "I've learnt my lesson. Appearances can be deceptive. Okay?"

It teased a smile from her. "Do you like the decor up here?"

"Love it. I'm transported back to a time when life was more simple. Very relaxing."

They finished their first course and Jodie cleared it away before they resumed conversation.

"What happened to your mother, Christine?" Shane asked quietly.

"She died of viral pneumonia seven months ago."

"You must miss her very much."

"I do. She was a warm and wonderful person." Her eyes hardened with belligerent pride. "Honest, hardworking and generous to a fault. She may only have been a barmaid, but she brightened a lot of people's lives."

Shane considered her intently for several seconds before softly asking, "Why *only*, Christine? Has someone criticised your mother for *only* being a bar-maid?''

"Some people consider a barmaid socially unac-ceptable,'' she said tightly, holding in her bitter anger.

The dark eyes bored into hers. "Like who?''

"Like a doctor I was going out with,'' she an-swered, defiantly holding her gaze steady on his. "I thought he was serious about me. So did my mother. She was so happy to think of me marrying a doctor. It was like a fulfilment of all she'd done, giving me the best she could. My mother always had great dreams for me. She wanted me to have everything in life that she hadn't had.''

"But the doctor didn't marry you.''

"No. He took me home with him to meet his fam-ily. They were very smooth, wealthy people,'' Chris-tine drawled with acid emphasis. "They didn't think I would make a suitable wife for their son. His ardour cooled after they made their judgement obvious. To me and to him.''

"He was a wimp.''

The fine contempt in Shane's voice surprised her. "I thought so, too. When it became clear that he was not going to thumb his nose at his family's opinion, I told him he was wasting my time and to clear out of my life.''

"Good riddance.''

Christine looked at him curiously. Was it a pose of approval, or were his remarks genuinely felt? "What about your family?'' she asked bluntly. "Would they approve if you took up with a woman of my kind of background?''

"No, they wouldn't." A hard ruthlessness glittered in his eyes, and his mouth curled into a cruel little smile. "But the difference is I wouldn't care, Christine. In fact, I'd enjoy shoving it right up their noses."

Was that the purpose he had in mind for her? Did flouting his family give him some deep bitter satisfaction? She remembered the sardonic tone he had used in speaking of his grandfather. One thing was certain. He might have made himself independent of his family, but he was not free of them. The fact that he had come to see his grandfather in hospital was proof of that.

His face relaxed into a more receptive expression, his eyes twinkling interest at her. "Why did you become a nurse?"

"Because I like caring for people. It's good to feel you're making a bad time easier for them. Helping them get well again."

He smiled approval. "What part of St. Vincent's has your services?"

That was a tricky question. Christine didn't want to lie, but she did not yet want to reveal that his grandfather was one of the patients who had her services.

"There are so many wards there," she answered slowly, then decided to use Shane Courtney's technique against him. "I move around."

Jodie provided a timely distraction by returning with their main course, and again the conversation lapsed except for inconsequential comments while they ate.

The sea perch was perfectly cooked, the French fries were fat and crisp, and the accompanying salad was tasty and generous.

Shane insisted that they order sweets, as well, his eyes lighting up when he saw bread and butter pudding on the menu. "Haven't had that since boarding school."

"Why were you sent to boarding school?"

"It was an effective way of getting rid of me."

The bald statement was made all the more shocking by the careless tone of its delivery. Christine couldn't let it go unquestioned. "You weren't wanted?"

"No. I was never wanted." His eyes mocked her shock. "It wasn't totally bad," he said. "It taught me to stand alone. Be independent. And to do what I consider is right, regardless of the opinion of others."

No wonder he felt a ready sympathy for her mother. *Abandoned by those who should have cared.* And he surely had first-hand experience of mean hearts. Her green eyes darkened with compassion. "You must have felt terribly alone."

He shrugged. "I survived." The dark pride in his eyes denied any want or need for pity.

"What about your grandfather?" she asked impulsively. "Didn't he care for you?"

"As I grew older, he seemed to like me more." There was a grim hardness in his voice as he added, "But then he put me in an untenable position. Unlike some simpering sycophants I could name, I walked out on him. He wasn't going to turn me into one of them."

"But you still came to visit him," Christine pressed, wanting to understand the situation.

His mouth twisted. "Yes. I did. Call it one last chance to find a meeting ground. Probably futile."

He leaned forward and pressed her hand, his eyes burning with intensity. "Forget my family. It's you I'm interested in, Christine. You I want to know about. Tell me more about your life with your mother. The happy times you had together."

Christine sensed a hunger in him to know everything about the kind of upbringing she had experienced. She responded automatically, conscious that she had been given far more than Shane despite all his material advantages from having been born into a wealthy family.

He kept drawing her out, and she found his interest more and more exhilarating. He seemed absorbed in each change of expression on her face, as though she was the most fascinating woman he had ever met. There were many moments of shared amusement when his dark eyes caressed her with a warm intimacy that squeezed her heart. Certainly his ardour wasn't cooled by being confronted with the world she lived in.

Eventually the live band that entertained in the bar downstairs on Sunday afternoons started up. Shane seemed to listen with pleasure to the old Irish folk songs. They stayed until the restaurant closed at 3 p.m., by which time the crowd below was much noisier, joining in the singing with rollicking enthusiasm.

Mike Donovan, the main vocalist in the band, spotted Christine as she came downstairs. He was a big bear of a man with a beard and a ponytail and a huge barrel chest. He looked an absolute ruffian, but his face always beamed good humour.

"Here's me darlin'," he crooned into the microphone. "Let's have Christine's song."

The band instantly swung into the tune to a loud chorus of approval from the audience. Mike switched to his *Bing Crosby* voice and beckoned Christine forward so he could sing directly to her.

When Irish eyes are smiling
Sure 'tis like a morn in spring,
In the lilt of Irish laughter
You can hear the angels sing.

She smiled at Shane, who had moved to her side. "True," he murmured in her ear, sliding his hand around her waist to draw her close to him.

When Irish hearts are happy
All the world seems bright and gay
And when Irish eyes are smiling...

Mike's eyes twinkled at both of them as he held on to the note, then looked directly at Shane as he sang the last line.

Sure they'll steal your heart away.

In the roar of applause that followed, Christine found herself blushing furiously. Shane, however, hugged her closer to him, apparently enjoying the spotlight that had been turned upon them.

Mike winked at him. "She's a great girl, mate. Look after her."

"No worries, mate," Shane replied in kind.

"Rose's song," someone yelled out.

The cry was taken up. "Yeah! Sing Rose's song!"

"A chorus for your mum, Christine," Mike said softly.

The band struck up the tune and Mike lifted his voice high. "My wild Irish Rose..."

The whole crowd joined in with sentimental fervour.

The sweetest flower that grows
You may search everywhere
But none can compare
With my wild Irish Rose.

Christine had to fight back a rush of tears at the memories the song evoked and the strong affection with which her mother was remembered by others. "Thanks, Mike," she said huskily when the song had ended, then managed a wobbly smile at Shane. "Let's go now."

He swept her through the crowd, acknowledging the well wishes called after them with a royal salute, as though he were a prince escorting a princess past her loyal subjects. People laughingly made way for them, enjoying the act, and only when they emerged from the hotel did Shane drop his protective and possessive hold on Christine.

He smiled at her as he removed his arm from her waist and captured her hand in his for companionable walking. "Thank you for taking me there. For sharing so much with me," he said warmly, and Christine could no longer find it in her heart to deny the closeness he was pressing. She wanted it, as well.

They did not talk on the way home. Christine swung between a wild exultation that the sense of togetherness was real, and a fear that she might be living in a fool's paradise. The man beside her was too perfect. Surely there had to be flaws somewhere, hidden away in his dark background that he seemed intent on leaving dark. Yet perhaps it was better to turn one's back on a hurtful past and build a completely new life. He had passed all her tests with flying colours. What more could she ask?

Nevertheless, when they reached her gate and Shane opened it for her, a host of reservations jabbed into Christine's mind. She made her feet step onto her front porch, but as the gate clanged shut behind them, she shot a searching glance at Shane, her heart skittering nervously at the thought of being alone in the house with him.

She wanted to know what it was like to be kissed by him. But would he leave it at that?

There was a look of intense satisfaction on his face as he took a key from his jeans pocket and smoothly unlocked and opened the front door for her. Christine hesitated, unsure about what she wanted to happen next. Shane drew her inside, having no hesitation whatsoever about what he wanted to happen next.

The moment the front door was shut on the outside world, he turned to her and invitingly said, "Come upstairs with me."

Christine's mind instantly whirled into a panicky spin. "I don't think..."

"I want to show you something."

Her heart did a double loop as she stared at his persuasive smile, wildly thinking he could probably persuade her into anything once he started. Some tempting strain of logic in her mind argued that a perfect man would surely be a perfect lover. Another more sober strain insisted she keep him at arm's length. At least for a while.

"No," she said.

He frowned at her. "I want to make some changes upstairs."

"Then do it. Rearrange however you like."

"I need you to see—"

"No!"

The charm fell from his face. He released Christine's hand and turned to confront her, suddenly emitting the formidable air of a controlled but ruthless decision maker.

"I didn't take you for a coward, Christine," he stated, the dark eyes burning with a deep and unrelenting challenge.

Her chin instinctively lifted. "I'm not. Nor am I a fool, Shane Courtney."

"People who shillyshally when the obvious is staring them in the face end up losers."

"People who hide their heads in the sand end up losers, too," she retorted.

"What do you gain by running away from what's between us?" His eyes glittered mockingly. "Do you want to lie and say there's nothing?"

"No. But I don't know you very well," she replied stubbornly.

"Then I'll give you my philosophy. When a current is flowing this strongly, you ride it. You seize the day, Christine. Hesitate too long, and the boat is gone, not waiting for time and tide to change."

Her green eyes flashed proud defiance. "I can find another boat."

His mouth curled sardonically. "Sure you can. My grandfather stuck to what he considered a safe steady boat, and now he's got a shipwreck on his hands. But he's like you. He'd rather choke on his lonely pride than admit it."

"I'm not denying I find you attractive," she defended.

"So when do you stop rejecting me on the basis of what the wimpish doctor did?"

A painful flush swept her cheeks. She could not defend that accusation. It was precisely what she had been doing since Shane had first approached her.

"It's not my way to fight on with losing battles, Christine," he continued, hammering the point into her heart. "Particularly where people insist on remaining blind. I cut losses and find winnable ground."

He paused, waiting for her response.

She had none. She was churning over the way she had been fighting his attraction all day, making him prove he was worthy of her interest. He had done nothing wrong. All he had done was pursue his interest in her at considerable cost to himself. It was she who had kept leaping to prejudicial conclusions.

"Have a think about it," he advised. "In the meantime, I'll visit my grandfather. Who may have cleared his throat of the deadwood by now."

He strode to the front door, opened it, then gave her a mocking salute as he closed it behind him.

CHAPTER FIVE

SHANE DID NOT COME BACK until well after visiting hours closed. Christine's body was wound tight. She had been listening for his return since eight o'clock, sitting on the sofa under her window, making desultory attempts at reading her library book.

It was now nine, and since Shane had left this afternoon, she had found it impossible to concentrate on anything. She had fumed about his arrogance, defended her caution, worried herself sick over whether he had already cut his losses with her, told herself she didn't care.

But she did care.

She was acutely conscious of her quickened heartbeat when his footsteps paused in the hallway. Of course, he would have seen the light from her window. He knew she was still up and awake. He knocked, a couple of quick raps that sounded more indifferent than determined.

"Yes?" she called out, her voice too sharply eager.

"Are you decent?" came the dry inquiry.

"Yes." She had been far too distracted to think of changing her clothes or getting ready for bed.

He opened the door without asking for permission, but he didn't come in. He leaned his right shoulder against the doorjamb, his gaze unerringly targeting Christine where she sat with her long legs curled up on the sofa. She stared at him, her heart contracting from the sheer power of his presence. Tension whipped between them as he held her gaze, silently challenging the distance she made no move to close.

Christine knew this was decision time. Shane Courtney thought of himself as a winner. There was only so much rejection he would countenance before he retreated. That was true of all people, Christine thought. No interest could grow without encouragement. It was probably more true of Shane, given the rejection he had known from his childhood.

He had reached out to her today, possibly in a way he reserved for very few people. The distance he kept now spelled out that he was perfectly prepared to stand alone. It was nothing new to him. The choice was hers.

"I'm not running away from you, Shane," she said in a nervous rush. "But I am scared. Not so much of being involved with you, but where it will end."

"It can have no end without a beginning, Christine," he said softly, then shrugged himself upright and strolled towards her. "I'm glad you waited up for me."

The purpose emanating from him started a flutter in her stomach. "I was reading a book," she said weakly.

"Is it a good book?" He gave her a quizzical little smile as he casually hitched himself onto the wide armrest of the sofa.

"I..." Christine swallowed hard, acutely aware of the powerful male thigh so close to her arm. "It's all right," she forced out.

"Where is the line drawn in your mind, Christine?" he asked softly. "Do you know?"

She jerked her gaze up to his. "I'm not sure what you mean."

"Didn't you wait up for me to see where it might lead?" He looked at where her hand was resting on the opened pages and slowly placed his hand next to it. "To see what happened," he murmured, "if a finger met a finger."

Christine watched in mesmerised fascination as he matched action to words. It was only the merest touch, yet her whole body was concentrated on feeling it.

"And another finger met another finger...and another met another," he mused in a hypnotic tone, his hand lightly edging over hers with a seductive artistry that kept her totally in thrall. Until he looked up and captured her eyes with piercing intensity. "Where might it lead?"

It jolted Christine into snatching her hand away. "It mightn't lead anywhere!" Yet her heart was racing, and the depth of her disturbance showed in the flush rising to her cheeks.

There was no longer any doubt that Shane Courtney had made his decision, and he was now advancing on every front. The removal of her hand was no deterrent at all.

"What would you do," he asked, "if you were a man, and you saw a lovely woman, wild, passionate, full of life, and she had a strand of hair not quite correctly placed? Would you do as I do—" his hand lifted and softly raked a wayward tress behind her ear "—so that she looked absolutely perfect to you?"

Christine took a deep breath. He was incredibly skilful at weaving a sensual spell, and every defensive instinct cried out for her to break it now, before she proved hopelessly vulnerable to it. Yet she did not want to.

Shane swung himself off the armrest and was suddenly down on one knee in front of her, taking both her hands in his, galvanising her attention on him.

"Are you interested, Christine? Are you intrigued? Do you want to draw the line now? Or do you want to explore more?"

The intensity flowing from him curled around her, bonding her to the moment of truth he was pressing upon her. She had never had a man on his knee to her, yet there was nothing of the petitioner in Shane Courtney. If anything, it increased his personal forcefulness that he could take up such a position and still emanate a dominating control over what would ensue from it.

"To see what it leads to," he urged softly. "The decision is yours as much as mine, Christine."

"What have you decided in your mind, Shane?" she asked, frantically clamping down on her turbulent feelings.

"I've decided the direction of my future. And I want to know what part of it you can, or will, share with me, Christine. Call it the crossroads. Do you want to come with me?"

He radiated purpose and conviction, and the tug of so much strength was wellnigh irresistible. It would be so easy to be carried along with him, letting him lead her to whatever he willed.

"We hardly know each other," she said, leaning forward in her earnest need for him to understand the dilemma in her mind.

"Then this is an opportunity to learn what we both want to know."

He released one of her hands to lift his to her face, softly cupping her cheek. Christine stared at him in fascinated anticipation as he leaned forward, his eyes inviting, compelling her compliance to his mouth reaching across the intervening space and finding her lips. He gently tilted her chin. It was so slowly and deliberately done, Christine knew he was giving her the chance to draw back. She didn't want to. She waited in trembling submissiveness, neither retreating nor moving forward to meet him. He had to come the full distance to her.

The touch of his mouth was as soft as thistledown, sending sensitive tingles over her lips. He didn't take. He didn't give. He tasted her as though she were a million-dollar bottle of champagne, and the bubbles excited him. His head bent to one side, but there was no pressure to force her to the cushioned support of the sofa. The touch was too exquisite for movement. Like being held in a vacuum, every contact mattered.

He moved around her mouth like an explorer in a new world where everything he found was like nothing he had known before. The fingers of his right hand slid between the fingers of her left in an intertwining embrace that he lifted and held to his chest, drawing it to his heart, savouring it.

The soft mobility of his mouth caressed and teased the voluptuous softness of her own. His other hand drifted from her chin to curl around the nape of her neck, fingers gently stroking, finding a nerve that sent sharp tingles to the base of her spine. Christine shivered.

He moved to slide his arms around her waist, lifting her to hold her close, drawing her off the sofa to stand upright with him, her body pressed lightly to his in an embrace that forced nothing from her. Whenever she wanted to pull away, she could. He was not out to frighten or pressure her. She could let what was happening happen, or not. Whatever pleased her. Christine knew this in part of her mind, but the rest of her was held in thrall to the exploring of more of the unknown.

His mouth continued to part her lips farther and farther, enveloping them with his own, imparting a sweet, swaying rhythm that she felt in his body, through her breasts, her nipples tightening with excitement as they brushed against his chest. The tantalising sensual movement drew her into leaning closer to him.

A hand stroked up and down the deep cleft of her spine, circled the pit of her back, came to rest below her hips, pressing her lower body to meet his. Christine had never felt such an electric awareness of her femininity as she did at coming into contact with the hard maleness of Shane's thighs, feeling the softness of her own giving against the masculine tautness of his. A quiver of primitive vulnerability rippled through her.

Again his right hand took possession of her left one, fingers interlacing in a tight grip as he held it behind her. It had nothing to do with inducing submission. Christine knew intuitively that Shane Courtney had no need of that from any woman. Rather it was the feeling of intimacy, of being part of one another, of interlocking contact, the sensual contact where one body merged with another into unity.

It was another expression of the way he was kissing her now, his mouth entwining with hers, deeper and deeper, seductively mingling invasion with sensitivity, weaving a magical web of complete and utter possession that melted any inclination to break free. It was beautiful. Mind spinning. The involvement was so intense Christine lost all sense of caution.

It was the hardening pressure of his arousal against the base of her stomach that finally jolted her to the reality of the situation. Yet even then she lost a struggle against the tempting excitement of knowing the full strength of his virility. The aggressive thrust of his maleness grew harder and harder against her, arousing desires that Christine had never before experienced. For several wild, wanton moments she revelled in her female power to draw this urgent desire from him.

There could be very little doubt of Shane's need for sexual appeasement. His body was tautly tuned for it, and the thought of having this impressively aroused man naked against her made Christine's insides squirm with excitement.

Before she knew what she was doing, her hips were moving, savouring a more sensuous range of contact, her free hand was curling around his neck, inciting a more passionate possession of their mouths, and her breasts were pushing hard against the warm wall of his chest, wanting more and more sensation.

It was sheer and utter madness. Control was irretrievably lost as Shane released her hand, his arms sweeping her tightly against him, rubbing her body against his, arching her back, seeking more vibrant pleasure in the giving softness of her body. A groan of intense need erupted from his lips as their mouths separated. He started lowering her towards the floor.

"What are you doing?" she cried, a stark cold wash of sanity flooding over her fevered foolishness.

A look of sheer and utter disbelief clouded his eyes before he could recollect where he was. He sucked in a quick breath and brought her upright, steadying her before easing himself slightly away from her. He lifted a hand to her temple, his fingers attempting a soothing touch, trailing a light reassurance down her cheek.

"I was merely trying..." he started gruffly, stopped to swallow hard, stretched his mouth into a smile of ironic humour. Except there was not the slightest trace of humour in his eyes. "I was merely trying to find out," he continued, forcing a lighter tone into his voice, "what it would be like...to come home to you...every evening of my life."

"You believe..." Christine's voice was little more than a croak. She was flushed, trembling. She did her best to work some moisture into her mouth, which was still tingling from the taste of his. "You believe in finding out everything as quickly as you can, do you?" she pushed out with as much bravado as she could manage, achingly conscious of having been a more than willing partner in the experiment. If it could be called that.

His chest heaved as he scooped in a deeper breath. There was still a slightly glazed look in his eyes, bright and glittery and not quite back to the sharply controlled intelligence that had demanded a decision from her.

"It seemed—" he paused to search for the right word "—appropriate for us both to know. Don't you think?"

"I think...I think..." Christine shook her head in wretched confusion. "I don't know what to think."

How could she have acted like that? Inviting. Inciting. Not even with Alan, whom she thought she would marry, had she ever felt so aroused and excited. In all fairness she could not blame Shane for what had almost happened. Her complicity had been too complete to blame him for anything. She was intensely grateful that he was allowing her a reasonably dignified recovery.

"I'm not usually like that," she offered in pleading excuse, her eyes begging some leeway from him for her behaviour.

He gave a sigh of regretful resignation. "Do I take it you've drawn the line for tonight?"

"Yes." She clutched at the line he'd handed to her, relieved that he was making her withdrawal so easy.

He suddenly grinned. "If you want to change your mind, I promise I'll still respect you in the morning."

It teased a rueful smile from her. "I don't imagine you care about that."

"True. I'd rather make love to you now. And in the morning."

The glittery darkness of his eyes promised an ardour to match his virility, and Christine felt her stomach clench in sheer physical yearning for what he promised. The response he had drawn from her was still pulsing in painful frustration, and it was totally futile to argue that sex without love could not be truly satisfying. Whether she loved him or not, she could not deny that she wanted to know every intimacy with Shane Courtney.

Sheer devilment danced into his eyes. "I really need you to come upstairs with me. To show you what changes I want to make to the rooms."

"At the price you're paying for them, you can make what changes you like," she said dryly.

One eyebrow lifted quizzically. "You're giving me carte blanche?"

"So long as you don't knock walls down."

He grimaced in mock disappointment. "You're determined on saying good night to me here and now."

"Yes."

He softly raked her bangs aside while his eyes simmered into hers. "You are very beautiful . . . and very desirable, Christine."

Then he kissed her again, and the kiss went on for a very long time before Christine could bring herself to break away, clinging weakly to some self-respect despite knowing it was hanging on a very thin thread in the face of Shane Courtney's determined advance.

"Good night, Shane." She rushed out the words shakily, then pushed herself away from him, not trusting herself to resist his attraction any more firmly than she had before.

He made no further attempt to bend the line his way. He nodded, accepting her decision, then slowly backed off and walked to the doorway. There he turned, his eyes skating over her body as though memorising it for his dreams. His gaze finally flicked to hers, and the dark eyes burned with deep satisfaction.

Then in a soft voice that sheathed ruthless purpose in seductive velvet, he said, "Knocking down walls is precisely what I intend to do, Christine."

CHAPTER SIX

IT WAS NOT one of the General's good days.

Christine had to admit that Shane's sardonic name for his grandfather fitted Max Courtney like a glove. However, when she took in his medication on Monday morning, Max had clearly withdrawn his leadership from the rank and file in the ward. *Brooding* was the word that sprang to mind.

He did not return her smile.

"Bad night?" she asked sympathetically.

His mouth twisted into a disgruntled grimace. "Ah, Sunshine." He had given her that name on his first day in the ward, declaring her sunny smile was enough to brighten anyone's day. "What's the use of having a heart attack if you can't get your own way from it?"

Her green eyes twinkled knowingly. "I would have thought you did a fair job of getting your own way, Max."

He heaved a sigh. "Not with my grandson." His dark eyes—eyes exactly like Shane's—glared frustration at her. "He's been corrupting the nurses all weekend. Giving them cherries. Mushing them up with his smile."

"So I've heard," Christine said, amused by what sounded like the tone of a sulky little boy. "When I came on shift this morning, the night staff reported that your grandson was a gorgeous hunk, and there were still some cherries left in the staffroom."

"Hmph!" It was a derisive snort. "He might be a handsome devil, Sunshine, but he's hard as nails. Harder!"

Not completely, Christine thought. Shane certainly went after what he wanted, but he had been fair about not forcing her beyond where she wanted to go. How long she could keep up her protective walls was, however, highly questionable. His departing declaration last night had left her in no doubt as to his intentions, and Christine could not deny she was very interested, and intrigued, to see where it would lead.

Having filled Max's cup with water, she passed it to him and tipped his pills from the plastic container into his hand. "These should help make you feel better," she said brightly, flashing him another smile.

"The only thing that will make me feel better is winning," he grumbled.

"Winning what?" she asked, curious to know what was transpiring between Shane and his grandfather.

He stared at the pills in his hand. "Shouldn't take these," he muttered. "It took a heart attack to bring that stubborn young buck back to me. If I had another attack..."

"You'd be dead. And that won't win anything for you," Christine dryly advised.

"Damn it, Sunshine! There's got to be a way."

The look of determination on his face had the same stamp of ruthless steel she had seen on Shane's. An image flashed into Christine's mind of two bulls locking horns together, fighting for supremacy.

"Take your pills, Max," she insisted. "I'll have to call the registrar if you don't. There are plenty of other people waiting for this hospital bed, you know. People who want to get better."

He winced and tossed the pills into his mouth, washing them down with a gulp of water. His brows were lowered over sharply mocking eyes as he gave her the plastic cup. "That smile of yours covers the soul of a gestapo commandant. You like getting your own way too, Sunshine."

She grinned. "All for your own good, Max."

He settled back on his pillows with a heavy sigh. "I mucked things up, Sunshine. When you get to my age and you see time running out on you, you want to make things right." He gave her a rueful smile. "Right for me, anyway."

"Everybody wants that, Max," Christine responded. "For things to be right for them."

She wanted whatever happened with Shane Courtney to turn out right for her, but there was obviously some conflict going on between him and his grandfather that could influence that outcome. Christine could not completely erase her wariness about wealthy families, despite Shane's assurances. Max Courtney liked her as a nurse, but would he approve of her as a woman of any importance in his grandson's life?

Max seemed to be brooding over her words. "I can't make it right for him. What's gone is gone. And he won't forgive, Sunshine. Or forget."

Christine frowned. "Do you mean your grandson?"

"Hard as nails," he affirmed. "Won't give an inch."

"He came to see you. Surely that means..."

"It means he knows he's got me over a barrel." Max gave a harsh laugh. "I need him. But he doesn't need me. And he's letting me know it. Giving those cherries to you nurses..." His eyes filled with dry mockery. "Not sucking up to me like the rest of the family, is he?"

"Do you want him to?"

"No way! He's no vulture." He grimaced. "He's like me."

"Hard as nails?" Christine teased.

His grimace twitched into an appreciative grin. "Sharp as a tack, aren't you, Sunshine? But I'm an old man. With an ailing heart."

"Who maybe doesn't want to admit he's made mistakes," Christine said archly.

His eyes twinkled at her. "That's always weakness, Sunshine. Compromise is a word used by the devil."

She shrugged. "I've always thought it took a strong man to admit his mistakes."

He laughed. "You only do that when you're in an impregnable position and you can't be thrown out for them."

"Well, I guess you know what's best for you, Max," Christine tossed at him as she started moving the drug trolley on to the next patient. "To my mind, if you want to win forgiveness, you start admitting mistakes."

She felt his eyes boring into her back as she greeted the man in the next bed and asked about his weekend. There were six patients in the ward and Christine went to each one of them, dispensing medication and having a little chat as she did so. Yet all the time she was wondering if Max Courtney was considering her words.

It was probably stupid for her to have said them. She might have more chance of a future with Shane if he remained estranged from his grandfather. She had spoken out of her deep-rooted belief that if you had family, you didn't disown them. You could disagree, you could disapprove, but somewhere along the line, differences should be settled to allow the relationship to continue. No-one else could really take the place of family.

If Alan had loved her enough to stick by her, Christine believed that his family would have come around to accepting them as a couple in time. He had simply crumbled under the threat of losing their financial backing should he marry without their approval. She smiled over Max Courtney's description of his grandson. A man as hard as nails wouldn't crumble under any threat. He would go his own way.

But was Shane's way Christine's way?

What road had he decided to take last night?

With her?

And with his grandfather?

She glanced at Max Courtney as she left the ward. His eyes were closed, but his face did not have the look of peaceful sleep. His jaw was set in teeth-gritting determination. Christine suspected he was shutting out everything else to brood over strategy for the next meeting with his grandson, and undoubtedly it was winning that dominated his mind.

Shane arrived at eleven-thirty.

Christine had just entered the women's ward, about to start the rounds of checking charts and entering the new data that had to be written up. She heard his voice asking after his grandfather at the office and the responding brightness in the voices that answered him.

Christine had hoped Shane would come during her work shift. The opportunity to see whether he would own to an interest in her in front of his grandfather was now hers for the taking. If he did, she could see Max Courtney's reaction to it. It should settle part of the question of whether an involvement with Shane would bring hurt or happiness.

Of course, he would then know she had deliberately held back on telling him she had met his grandfather and seen his family. But he had held back on telling her quite a few things, also. Tit for tat, Christine thought, as she quickly worked her way around the ward, emanating brisk efficiency.

She told herself there was no hurry to catch Shane with his grandfather. Max Courtney was not the kind to rush into battle with an equally strong antagonist. The General would undoubtedly be probing for an opening that he could work to his advantage.

When she moved to the men's ward, the scene was precisely as she had anticipated. Shane was sitting on the far side of his grandfather's bed, in the armchair by the window. His eyes widened with surprise when he saw her. Christine knew she looked considerably different dressed in her nurse's uniform, with her long hair woven into a single plait from the crown of her head, but recognition was instant.

Several expressions flitted over his face before understanding produced a slow smile that seemed to appreciate the testing nature of the situation.

Having lost his grandson's attention, Max Courtney swung his head around to glare irritably at the source of distraction.

Christine returned a bright challenging smile to both of them as she moved straight down to their end of the ward. "I'll start with you today," she said, picking up Max's chart from the holder at the bottom of the bed.

Shane had risen to his feet, his dark eyes sparkling with devilish delight. "What an unexpected pleasure to see the ministering angel at work. I missed you this morning, Christine."

"The day shift starts at seven-fifteen," she informed him blithely.

"You two know each other?" Max demanded, frowning heavily at the thought that he might have slipped up in speaking his mind earlier this morning.

"We're living together," Shane declared, totally unconcerned about how such a term could be interpreted.

"He means we occupy the same house," Christine corrected with some asperity.

Max's frown grew heavier. "What's going on here that I don't know about?" he growled, looking suspiciously from one to the other. "What are you up to, Sunshine?"

"I'm going to take your temperature, your pulse and your blood pressure."

"They're already up," he said, heaving himself into a sitting position against his pillows and looking particularly pugnacious.

"You don't know when to give up," Shane said. "And you don't know when to lie down, either."

Max snorted. "The next thing she'll be asking me is if I've had my shower and been to the toilet."

"I do need those answers, Max," Christine said firmly. "Have you had your shower and opened your bowels?"

The General's fists slammed into the bedclothes. "All my life I've gone when I've wanted to go, and I don't go when I don't want to. And no-one's going to make me do any different."

"Oh, we can easily change that," Christine said sweetly.

"How can a man get better in conditions like this? They're trying to kill me. Hospitals are hell!" He looked outraged to his very soul as he turned in appeal to his grandson. "If you have any pity in your heart, get me out of here, Shane. Take me home."

Christine took the thermometer from the blue case attached to the wall and slid it under Max's tongue. "Let's make sure you're normal," she said reasonably.

"I'm not normal," he mumbled. "Never have been."

She took his wrist to check his pulse. The adrenalin was certainly flowing. His pulse was faster than normal. She entered it on the chart.

"Good or bad?" Shane asked.

"A little bit excited," Christine replied.

"I'd never have guessed," Shane said dryly.

"Stop discussing me in front of me," Max growled. "I'm not dead yet. And don't intend to be. So tell me the worst. What's going on between you two?"

"Nothing," said Christine.

"Everything," said Shane.

"He's upstairs, and I'm downstairs," Christine stated.

"A temporary hitch," said Shane. "I'm working on it."

"What's your full name?" Max shot at Christine.

"May I have the pleasure of introducing the woman in my life," Shane said mockingly. "Christine, this is my grandfather, Max Courtney. Grandfather, this is Christine Delaney."

Max frowned at her. "Delaney..." His eyes sharply reappraised her features as Christine went about preparing to check his blood pressure. "You're a very beautiful young woman."

"Shane keeps telling me the same thing," she said lightly.

"What have you two been doing together?" There was dark suspicion in his voice.

"Well, yesterday we went to Kitty O'Shea's Hotel for lunch," Shane tossed out casually. "It's up the road from Christine's house in Paddington."

"Why'd you go there?" Deep disapproval rasped through Max's voice. He subjected Christine to another hard, searching look as she fitted the band around his arm.

"Christine wanted to show it to me," Shane replied. He gave her a knowingly triumphant smile as he blandly added, "Her mother worked as a barmaid there for the last twenty years of her life."

Max made a choking sound. His face went bright red. He looked wildly at Christine, then at his grandson. "God damn you, Shane!" he burst out in bitter anger. "You're doing this to get at me. After all these years, to come back at me with this..."

Christine went cold at the outburst provoked by the revelation of her background.

"Max, you're putting up your blood pressure," she warned.

He waved his free arm in contemptuous dismissal. "Get that damned thing off me!"

"Don't speak to Christine like that. She's doing her job," Shane said with steely reproof. "Treat her with the same respect I do. She's not your servant."

"You're using her to spite me," Max accused.

"You made the bed you lie in, Grandfather," Shane said in icy contempt. "If you don't like it, do something constructive about it instead of sticking to your pig-headed prejudices. You can count on one certainty. Christine will not be a sacrifice to your ambitions for me."

"Shane, this arguing is too stressful for his heart," Christine pleaded, anxious for her patient's well-being.

"I'll decide that," Max snapped at her.

"No. *I* will," Shane said with arrogant command. "I'll leave you to reconsider your attitudes, Grandfather. When it comes to what's best for *my* personal life—" his eyes swept hotly over Christine. "—that's *my* decision, and mine alone."

Max glowered with rage. "Don't bother coming back."

"I won't." Shane glowered right back at him. "Not under any circumstances."

"Good!" said the old man. "I don't want you."

"Fine by me!"

Shane strode from the battle arena, leaving Christine to do what she could to calm down his grandfather. For which she was intensely grateful. No way in the world had she anticipated such a scene, and she was flooded with guilt for having put her personal interests in front of the well-being of a patient.

Max was breathing heavily, his face still flooded with bright colour, his eyes staring glazedly after his grandson.

"I'm sorry, Max. I didn't know," Christine rushed out in earnest apology. "I had no idea you'd be so upset. I met Shane by chance. It was only on Saturday, so—"

"By chance?" His gaze snapped to her, disbelief accusing her of lying. "Nothing that happens with Shane happens by chance."

"But it did. Completely by chance. I was at the bazaar. We were testing cherries together. He found out where I lived—"

"There! I told you so."

"Well, he had nothing to do with the fact that I had rooms to let."

"Grabbed his opportunity."

Christine heaved a defeated sigh. "Think what you like, Max. Now, please, let me take your blood pressure. It's bound to be high."

He relaxed on his pillows, not making any protest about it. He stared fixedly at her as she went through the procedure. His blood pressure was high, but not dangerously so. His breathing had steadied by the time she finished, and the high colour had drained from his face. He had the look of an old and tired warrior who should be retired from the field. A grimace of pain had him reaching for his angina tablets. Christine hastily provided him with one.

"You shouldn't get excited like this," she admonished. "You know it can only do you a damage."

"Chance," he repeated heavily. "Chance be damned!"

Despite his obvious disapproval of any relationship between her and his grandson, Christine could not feel any resentment towards the old man. It saddened her that people held such hurtful prejudices, and she wished the situation was different. As it was, she could not even feel any joy that Shane had stood up for his interest in her.

Max heaved a long, deep sigh, then offered her a twisted little smile. "You are very beautiful, Sunshine. If only things had been different..."

Christine wasn't sure what he meant. Was he referring to her background, or the ongoing conflict between himself and Shane? That obviously went back many years, and had to be rooted in very bitter differences of opinion that had torn them apart. Were still tearing them apart. Neither one of them was ready to back down on anything.

"I'm sorry," she said softly. "Try to relax and rest now, Max. I'll come to check your pressure again after I've finished with the other patients."

His eyes suddenly narrowed. "How do you feel about my grandson? Do you want him?"

"Max, I've only just met him," she protested, but she couldn't stop the self-conscious flush that betrayed her interest.

The old man closed his eyes. "It doesn't take long, Sunshine. Not long at all—" there was a sad reminiscent note in his voice "—but you can regret what you didn't do for the rest of your life."

CHAPTER SEVEN

CHRISTINE'S SHIFT ENDED at three forty-five. By four o'clock she was out of the hospital and trudging up the hill that led to her home. She hoped Max Courtney would not suffer any ill effects from the explosive scene with his grandson. It had worried her all afternoon, and still did.

She had worried about Shane, as well. Whatever had gone wrong between the two men went far deeper than any dispute over her. Max must have used the power of his position to demand too much from Shane, but Shane was absolutely wrong about his grandfather wanting to turn him into a simpering sycophant. *If* they could ever get past their mutual mulish pride, they might find a meeting ground, but Christine did not intend to become the meat in their sandwich while they chewed their way to the truce they both surely wanted.

How she was going to deal with Shane this evening was a more pressing matter to consider. Christine had no idea what she should say or do, but she was certain of one thing: Shane Courtney was not about to stop what he had started. Not after having declared in front of his grandfather that she was the woman in his life. Christine figured that hell would freeze over before

Shane backed down from pursuing his contentious interest in her.

But after today's revelations, did she still want to get involved with him?

Whether Shane's interest was genuine, Christine honestly didn't know. There was no doubt in her mind that he did desire her, but he could be using her to spite his grandfather. Grabbing an opportunity, as Max put it, to kill two birds with one stone by having a woman he fancied, while using her as a telling weapon in a family battle he was intent on winning.

Christine turned the corner into the cul-de-sac where she lived, still mulling over what to do about Shane. There was a truck parked in front of her house with a whole lot of building apparatus loaded onto it—ladders, a cement-mixer, tarpaulins, various tins of paint or whatever. She frowned, wondering why the truck was taking up her little space in the lane. Surely, if one of her neighbours was carrying out renovations, it would be more convenient to be parked where the work was being done.

Her feet faltered to a shocked halt when she saw a workman emerging from her front door. Another followed. Between them they carried a tarpaulin loaded with a smashed window and broken bricks. They had already closed the door and the gate behind them before Christine recovered enough to react.

"Hey!" she yelled, pushing her feet into a fast sprint up the lane. "Hey, you! That's my house!"

They swung the tarpaulin onto the tray of the truck, then turned to look curiously at her.

"What do you think you're doing?" Christine demanded.

"Cleaning up as ordered," one of them answered as she came panting up to confront them.

"This is my house and I didn't order anything!"

The other shrugged. "Too late now. All done. Better take it up with the guy inside. We just do what we're paid for, lady."

Shane! Horror zinged through Christine's mind. He *had* knocked down a wall! A real wall! She whirled towards the gate. "You won't get paid!" she shouted at the men, who looked after her in bemusement.

"We've been paid," one of them called to her.

How dared he! What incredible arrogance to just go ahead and knock down one of *her* walls! Never mind that she had said he could do what he liked. She had specifically told him he wasn't to knock down walls!

Christine was in such a fever of fury she could hardly get her key in the door. When she finally managed it, she hurled the door open, rushed inside and slammed it shut behind her, uncaring that it rattled the glass panels.

"Shane Courtney, where are you?" she yelled.

"Upstairs, of course," came the bland reply.

"You come on down here!" she commanded.

"Much better for you to come up here so you can see what I've done." Said with calm, inviting logic.

"Right!" she snapped. "I'm coming up."

There was dust everywhere. Christine could see the workmen's footsteps in it as she bounded up the stairs. Her heart quailed at the thought of what damage had been done to her house. The trail led to the back bedroom. She swung through the open doorway with murder in her heart, then came to a dead halt as she was hit by an unaccustomed stream of light.

Shane Courtney was standing in front of a window that was three times the size of the window that should have been there. "You see?" he said smugly. "Big improvement, isn't it?"

The view out over other terrace rows and tree-lined streets was quite mind-boggling at first. Then Christine noted that the wall around the window had been patched up and cement-rendered as before.

"Have to wait a couple of days for everything to dry properly before I get a painter in," Shane said matter-of-factly. "I reckon a soft gold colour. What do you think?"

Christine took a deep breath and let fly at him. "I think you've got a monstrous hide to go ahead behind my back and—"

"But I did ask you, Christine, and you said I could rearrange the rooms as I like," he reminded her.

"But not to knock walls down," she fired at him. "Not to..." Her tongue got into knots and she waved her hands helplessly at the window.

"It's only half a wall."

"Half—half..." Christine kept swallowing what she wanted to say, which was all jumbled up in her mind.

"What you need is a little time to get used to it," Shane said kindly. He came forward, reaching out to take her hands. "Come and sit down on the bed with me and—"

She flapped her hands at him and found her tongue again. "You get away from me, Shane Courtney. I'm not sitting on any bed with you. You're absolutely impossible!"

She stamped over to the window and turned her back on it as she hurled reproaches at him. "You go your own way. You take no consideration for anybody. First this morning with your grandfather. You couldn't leave the poor old man alone. You had to incite an argument—"

"That wasn't my fault," he protested, lifting his hands in appeal to her.

She planted hers firmly on her hips. "Whose fault was it, then?"

"Yours," he said. "You spelled it out quite clearly at Kitty O'Shea's. I wasn't about to let you down, Christine. I did precisely what you asked."

"*My* fault?" She couldn't believe he was blaming her.

"Yes, your fault," he insisted. "You wanted your background shoved up my family's noses. So I shoved it up my grandfather's."

"I didn't say that! You did!"

"Only putting your feelings into words," he pointed out. "In any event, it was you who was persecuting him with a thermometer and a sphygmomanometer, not to mention the ultimate humiliation of asking about his bowels.''

"It's my job to do that," Christine protested.

"I know. But *he* sees it as an invasion of privacy. And it put him in a position of weakness in front of me.''

"He is weak. And you ought to appreciate it instead of getting him upset.''

Shane threw up his hands. "I thought you'd be happy that I stood up for you and didn't back down.''

Christine shook her head helplessly, feeling a niggle of guilt at her participation in what had happened. But it wasn't really her fault. Shane must have known how his grandfather would react. As Max Courtney claimed, nothing with his grandson happened by chance. It had been another shot in the campaign to get his own way.

Her eyes filled with appeal. "Your grandfather *is* ill, Shane. Is winning worth the risk of bringing on another heart attack?''

"It's all right," he soothed. "Everything's out in the open now, with no harm done. I know you didn't mean to make trouble with my grandfather, Christine. Believe me. He makes it for himself. He's a stubborn old man who won't see the light.''

They were both stubborn. Flint striking off flint, Christine thought. And God help anyone who came between them.

Shane smiled away her concern and started towards her again. "Speaking of light, you're not really angry about the window, are you? You must admit it's a big improvement.''

"The cost—" she said weakly.

"—is mine. No problem for you, Christine. Though perhaps I should tell you there are a few other things I need to do to keep in touch with my office.''

"Like what?" she asked in alarm.

"Oh, some extra lines for a fax machine and access to the computer terminal. A couple of telephone lines. Now that I've got enough light, I'll set my lap-top up in here and—"

"Why are you doing this, Shane?"

His hands closed gently around her shoulders as he looked deeply into her eyes. "I want to spend as much time as I can with you.''

"But why?" The intensity flowing from him wound around her heart, infiltrating all her defences. She searched his eyes in a desperate bid for the truth of what he felt for her. "Your grandfather insists that you're using me to spite him.''

"I can only imagine that's his guilty conscience talking, Christine,'' Shane answered smoothly.

"What does he feel guilty about?"

"Perhaps trying to rule my life in both professional and personal areas. He went too far on both counts.''

"You enjoyed telling him about me,'' she accused.

"Yes, I did. Because you were there. And it was a chance to prove to you that nothing was more important to me than what we can have together.''

"How can you mean that?" she cried. "Last night you were prepared to cut your losses with me."

"No. I simply needed you to accept what was already true for me."

"Then tell me what *is* true for you, Shane," she pleaded.

"Christine..." He spoke her name as though it were soft, beautiful music in his soul. "I saw you, and it was like seeing a star I had to follow. Suddenly I knew what all the songs were about. A stranger across a crowded room, a magic moment, heart-turning, mind-bending, compelling..."

His hands slid from her shoulders and moved slowly, caressingly, up her long throat to cup her face. Christine held her breath, mesmerised by hearing him say what she had felt on seeing him.

"So I followed the star," he continued, his voice lowered to a hypnotic whisper that thrummed through her ears in tune with her quickened pulse. "And it grew brighter as I sought to find out more about it. Brighter and more beautiful. More compelling. I had to stay with it. Had to see where it led. Because it promised so much. And every step I took promised more—"

He bent his head and lightly brushed his lips over hers "—and more. I want more, Christine," he murmured, then slid his tongue seductively between her lips, arousing a sensitivity that craved her surrender to all he wanted.

Christine had no recollection afterwards of actually making a choice. She remembered the feeling of her whole body poised, shimmering with intense inner excitement, wanting to go wherever Shane led. She stopped thinking of anything. Her mind was filled with an awed wonder that this should be happening to her. It was the magic that dreams were made of. From which fantasies were woven.

Shane touched her so exquisitely. He kissed her as though he worshipped all she was with a vibrant intensity that hummed through her whole body in waves of sweet exultation. He made her feel alluringly perfect as he slowly undressed her.

Then seeing him undressed. Christine would never forget that moment as long as she lived. There could be no other man as magnificently made as Shane Courtney. He was the perfect embodiment of maleness. So strong and sure of himself. Sleekly beautiful and stunningly virile. She stared at him in glazed fascination, wildly anticipating how it would feel to take him inside her, to be filled by so much.

She had wanted him then. Right then and there. Wanted with a desire so powerful and overwhelming that Christine didn't know herself. It was as though she had turned into some other woman whose whole being was focussed on physical pleasure. Yet that didn't matter. Only what she was going to share with Shane mattered.

Nothing else existed. Not the past, not the future. No sense of danger, of caution or commitment. They were simply man and woman, about to come together in a climactic union, and the enthralling anticipation of that moment obliterated everything else.

Yet it didn't happen then. And that was right, too. They explored each other with touch, as though mutually attuned to a sense of ceremony, knowing that this time would never come again for them, wanting to savour every fine nuance of the experience, the sensation of newness, of an ultimate beginning for all there could be between them. If nothing else, a memory created and stored with loving care for every minute detail.

There was magic in their fingertips, magic in their lips, magic tingling over their skin, magic in their hearts. They moved to the bed in a fluid, floating dance of intense sensuality and slid into another movement, rolling over and over, luxuriating in every excitement of full body contact.

Shane untwined her plait, spreading her hair out on the pillows, winding it around himself as he kissed her with increasingly ardent passion. And Christine wound her arms around him, under his and over the tightened muscles of his back, bonding him ever closer to her.

Their legs entwined, slid apart, invited, incited what had to come, heightening their awareness of it to a tumultuous fever pitch. Then there could be no more waiting for either of them. Christine arched her body to meet the need of his and found her own need met with body-shattering ecstasy as she felt him plummeting into her.

She heard an exultant cry spill from her lips, heard it echoed from his, felt herself being drawn into a vortex of sensation that swelled and contracted and swelled again, surging into ever mounting circles of excitement, exquisite tension melting sweetly into more exquisite tension, Shane pushing her farther and farther along a path of no return, taking her with him to the outermost reaches of total intimacy where there was no sense of self, only one entity constantly merging, flowing, forming, complete unto itself. Utterly complete in the climactic mingling of all they gave to each other.

To have known this...

It filled Christine's mind with incredulous wonder as Shane lovingly cradled her through the long aftermath of ecstatic togetherness. She had never imagined there could be such all-pervasive fulfilment in being a woman with the right man. She had simply accepted her previous experience as all that there was, and been reasonably content in that acceptance. But there had been so much more to feel. A vivid never-to-be-forgotten kaleidoscope of depths and dimensions that lifted her consciousness of life to a wildly exhilarating vibrancy.

Shane... His name was a song in her heart, a symphony in her body, a blissful peace in her soul. The perfect man. The perfect lover.

Even now she could not bring herself to think about the future, could not bring herself to care. It was enough to have known this with him. More than enough.

Max Courtney's words slid into her mind. *You can regret what you didn't do for the rest of your life.*

Christine had no regrets over what she had done. If it led nowhere at all, it was still something to remember for the rest of her life.

GET A FREE TEDDY BEAR...

You'll love this plush, cuddly Teddy Bear, an adorable accessory for your dressing table, bookcase or desk. Measuring 5½" tall, he's soft and brown and has a bright red ribbon around his neck—he's completely captivating! And he's yours *absolutely free*, when you accept this no-risk offer!

AND FOUR FREE BOOKS!

Here's a chance to get **four free Harlequin Presents® novels** from the Harlequin Reader Service®—so you can see for yourself that we're like **no ordinary book club!**

We'll send you four free books... but you never have to buy anything or remain a member any longer than you choose. You could even accept the free books and cancel immediately. In that case, you'll owe nothing and be under **no obligation!**

Find out for yourself why thousands of readers enjoy receiving books by mail from the Harlequin Reader Service. They like the **convenience of home delivery...** they like getting the best new novels months before they're available in bookstores...and they love our **discount prices!**

Try us and see! Return this card promptly. We'll send your free books and a free Teddy Bear, under the terms explained on the back. We hope you'll want to remain with the reader service—but the choice is always yours!

106 CIH AJAW (U-H-P-05/93)

NAME

ADDRESS APT

CITY STATE ZIP

Offer not valid to current Harlequin Presents® subscribers. All orders subject to approval.
© 1993 HARLEQUIN ENTERPRISES LIMITED
Printed in the U.S.A.

▶ CLAIM YOUR FREE BOOKS AND FREE GIFT! RETURN THIS CARD TODAY! ▶

NO OBLIGATION TO BUY!

THE HARLEQUIN READER SERVICE: HERE'S HOW IT WORKS

Accepting free books puts you under no obligation to buy anything. You may keep the books and gift and return the shipping statement marked "cancel." If you do not cancel, about a month later we will send you 6 additional novels, and bill you just $2.24 each plus 25¢ delivery and applicable sales tax, if any*. That's the complete price—and compared to cover prices of $2.89 each—quite a bargain! You may cancel at any time, but if you choose to continue, every month we'll send you 6 more books, which you may either purchase at the discount price . . . or return at our expense and cancel your subscription.

* Terms and prices subject to change without notice.
  Sales tax applicable in N.Y.

CHAPTER EIGHT

THERE WAS A LILT of blissful happiness in Christine's step as she set out for the hospital the next morning. Shane's last kiss at the front door was still tingling on her lips. The sun was shining. And the world was a beautiful place. She danced a pirouette from sheer joy, uncaring if anyone watching thought her quite mad. Which she was. Madly in love with Shane Courtney.

She hugged herself, scarcely able to believe how perfect it had all been. Making love, sitting out in the garden of the Italian restaurant Shane had taken her to, their senses so alive that the meal they had eaten had tasted more delicious than any other, the champagne a heady delight, neither of them able to stop touching each other, making love with their eyes, then going home to share that wonderful intimacy again, lying in bed together, watching the stars come out through the new picture window.

Laughter bubbled from deep inside Christine. Shane had known exactly what he was doing in knocking down her wall. He might declare it was to let in the light, but as a way to get her upstairs with him it had definitely been a winning stroke. She no longer wanted any walls between them.

It seemed totally irrelevant to talk of the future. With a sense of freedom she had never known before, Christine thought that somewhere along the line the future would take care of itself. Shane was not about to leave her. He was staying.

Today the Telecom men were coming to put in the new lines. A cleaning service would set the house to rights again. Tomorrow the painters. Then the delivery of the office furniture Shane needed. He certainly had no intentions of being a fly-by-night lover.

Not even the thought of Shane's family could dim Christine's exhilaration. They would both rise above any disapproval aimed at them. She was so sure of it that the prospect of meeting any of the Courtneys held no worries for her.

However, she did check that Max Courtney had spent a trouble-free night as soon as she arrived at work. With that niggling concern off her mind, Christine sailed through her morning routine, spreading cheer around the wards with her infectious happiness. All the patients smiled at her. Even Max. Although his smile had a grudging edge to it.

"Glowing more than usual, Sunshine," he remarked.

"It's great to be alive," she chirped at him as she passed him his medication.

"What's Shane been up to?" he growled.

"Oh, smashing down a wall," she replied, her eyes twinkling with deliciously private pleasure.

"What wall?" Max demanded to know.

"Well, it was really only half a wall," Christine gaily conceded. "Shane wanted a bigger window in one of the upstairs bedrooms so he could set up his work there."

"Figuring on staying, is he?"

"Yes." Christine's grin was a mile wide.

Max eyed it narrowly as he swallowed his pills. "So what's he doing today?" he asked when he'd finished gulping them down.

Christine shrugged blithely. "Fixing up some other things he wants done to make himself comfortable."

"Not coming here then?"

She gave him a reproving look. "You did tell him not to come back, Max."

He gave a disgruntled grimace. "Shane knows I didn't mean it."

"How can he know that?"

A pause for consideration, then a hopeful look. "You can tell him, Sunshine."

Christine laughed at him. "Oh, no, you don't, Max. You don't use me as the go-between. I had enough of the firing line yesterday. You didn't exactly make *me* feel good, you know."

He frowned. "I got it wrong. I can see that now." He tried an appeasing smile as she took his water cup from him. "You can forgive a sick old man one mistake, can't you, Sunshine?"

She eyed him consideringly. "*I* can, Max. But I can't speak for Shane."

His mouth turned down again as he sank back on the pillows. "Stubborn young buck," he muttered darkly. "Something's got to be done. And it will be."

Which meant trouble, Christine thought.

It didn't take her too long to find out what form the trouble was going to take. Shortly after the lunch hour she received a message from the back-up nurse that Max Courtney wished to speak to her on a very private matter of extreme urgency.

With apprehension in her heart, Christine proceeded to bed nine. The old warrior had the gleam of battle in his eyes.

"Draw the armchair up and sit down, Sunshine," he commanded, clearly in fine fighting fettle.

Christine eyed him suspiciously as she did as she was bidden. "I told you I was not going to act as a go-between, Max," she warned. "This had better not be about Shane."

"Nothing to do with him," he said airily. "Strictly private between you and me."

"Okay. I'm listening," she said, not quite trusting his word.

He leaned towards her conspiratorially. "You can see what's happening, Christine."

It was the first time he had used her proper name. Which immediately put Christine on red alert. The General thought he had a battle plan that would win what he wanted.

"This hospital is killing me," he continued earnestly. "I've got to get out of here. And I've got to get out fast."

"Max," she said patiently, "you'll die faster if you're not properly looked after. You could easily have another serious heart attack. You were lucky last time. If you hadn't been in Sydney, doing business in Elizabeth Street, and been brought straight here by ambulance through Casualty, you'd be dead right now. If you go home to the central coast, you may not be so lucky next time. You need proper care and attention. And you need to be close to emergency services."

"I've got that all thought out," Max said triumphantly. "What I need is my own private nurse."

"And you expect me to recommend somebody?"

He grinned at her. "Not somebody, Sunshine. You're *it*."

"Max," she expostulated, "there's no way!"

"What's Shane paying you at the present moment?" he asked.

A self-conscious flush started sweeping up her throat. "Well, if you must know, he's paying a thousand dollars a week to rent the upstairs rooms."

"I'll double that!" Max said, his eyes agleam with determined purpose. "You can throw Shane out. I'll rent the rooms, and I'll pay you two thousand a week to be my private nurse."

She stared at him in disbelief. "This is crazy!" she muttered.

But Max had the bit between his teeth and he charged forward. "I can pay double anything Shane can offer you. I can pay more. He's no match for me. He might be worth a million or two, but I'm worth *tens* of millions. I can outbid him any day. And as far as I'm concerned, you're worth it. You'll earn every cent."

"I'm sure I would," Christine said feelingly. "It'd be so dreadful having to put up with you every day, Max."

"Make it five thousand a week. And I promise I'll be nice to you."

"The answer, Max, is a very decisive no. I will not be bought like that," she added resentfully.

The dark eyes mocked her. "Why do you think Shane is paying you a thousand dollars a week?"

A fierce flush swept into her cheeks. "That's different."

"Because he's young and handsome and you're attracted to him?"

"Because he's genuine. And you're not, Max," she flashed at him. "Your offer is nothing but a devious strategy to get at Shane again."

"Maybe he does have a genuine interest in you," Max conceded. "But what if he hasn't, Sunshine? What if he's using you to get at me?"

"How can he be using me? For what purpose?" she asked, scorning Max's attempt at driving a wedge between them.

"Didn't you ask him why I was so angry yesterday?" he asked.

Christine's face tightened. "That was obvious, Max. You don't think I'm good enough for your grandson," she bit out, her eyes defying him to deny it.

His grimace held a load of irony. "You're more than good enough, Sunshine. That's not the point at all." His eyes softened with sympathy as he posed more questions. "What if he deliberately chose you for the purpose of balancing the scales with me? A payback for something that happened years ago?"

"That's nonsense, Max. I told you we met by chance," Christine retorted, angrily dismissing his innuendos.

"I bet Shane knew who you were, what you were and where you worked before he turned up at your house," Max shot at her.

"So what if he did?" Christine countered. "He didn't know I had anything to do with you or this ward. That came as a complete surprise to Shane yesterday. I know that for a fact, Max."

He raised a sceptical eyebrow. "He was here at the weekend. You think he didn't ask the staff about you when he gave them the cherries?"

Christine frowned over the insidious suggestion. Of course it was possible, yet Shane's surprise at seeing her here had surely been genuine. If he had already learnt where she worked, why ask her about it when they were lunching together on Sunday? Why pretend he hadn't known about her connection to his grandfather? There seemed no point in such a deception. Besides, the sequence of events made Max's argument irrelevant.

"That would have been after Shane rented the rooms in my house," she pointed out with some asperity.

Max's dark eyes flashed with derision. "It might have started by chance, Sunshine, but once inside your home, he'd see, he'd remember . . ." The sharpness left his eyes, as though his mind had drifted to another time and place.

"Remember what, Max?" Christine prompted quietly.

His attention snapped to her. "You've known Shane three days. I've known him all his life. You think I don't know how his mind works? What drives him?"

The question forced Christine to reconsider. How much had Gino told Shane about her? Could her situation have influenced his decision to pursue her?

Shane had certainly pressed his interest in her beyond any normal standards of courtship. His demand for a decision from her, his forceful dismissal of time to get to know each other better, his evasion of questions about his family background . . . Had she been stupidly gullible with him? Had she let a dream, and her own vulnerability to his attraction, lead her hopelessly astray?

Christine could feel her inner joy and certainty draining away as the doubts Max was seeding took root and grew. Perhaps everything had been too perfect to be true. Even yesterday. Had Shane deliberately set out to seduce her for some reason he was keeping hidden?

She remembered the look of ruthless purpose on his face after inspecting her upstairs rooms on Saturday, remembered his satisfaction on Sunday when he said he would enjoy shoving her background up his family's noses. Perhaps Max was right, and nothing Shane had done was by chance or on impulse. Yet although his involvement with her might have started out with premeditated purpose, surely he also had been caught up in the magic of their lovemaking. He couldn't pretend that kind of feeling, could he?

"What's the payback for?" Christine asked tightly, clinging to the memory of how it had been with Shane last night.

"Ask *him*, Sunshine," Max challenged, his dark eyes deadly serious. "Then weigh what he says and judge how it fits in with his genuine interest in you."

"Why should I take any notice of what you say, Max? Won't your private nurse offer be retracted the moment you win what you want from it?" she demanded sceptically.

"You want proof that it's genuine?" His gaze flicked to the other end of the ward. "You'll get it right now. Here come the vultures, all primed to peck some more out of me."

The two couples sweeping into the ward emitted wealth and snobbery. Clothed in designer dresses and custom-tailored suits, they did not deign to acknowledge the presence of any of the *common* patients in the ward.

On their very first visit last week they had made it clear to the staff they found it offensive that any member of *their* family, let alone its chief, should be in the public sector of the hospital. The fact that it provided the easiest access to every medical specialist was totally irrelevant to them. It was beneath them to come to such a place. Yet they could not afford to ignore the man who held the family purse strings. They were punctilious in pandering to him.

Christine tried to swallow her antagonism as she quickly appraised their faces. Which were Shane's parents? There was some family likeness in the two men, but neither of them could be definitely identified as Shane's father. The women were totally dissimilar, giving no clue whatsoever to any relationship with Shane.

Christine glanced at Max as she rose to her feet to make way for his visitors. The genes must have skipped a generation. The only real likeness to Shane was in the old man, who suddenly turned to her and grasped her hand, his dark eyes—Shane's eyes—sharply compelling.

"You stand by and watch this," he commanded. "See what I've got to put up with. How I could have had sons with mush for brains...?" He shook his head. "Might as well have rings through their noses the way their wives lead them around."

Christine felt no compunction to obey Max. It was curiosity that held her beside him, not his hand or his command. She simply wanted to know more about Shane's family and why he was so estranged from it.

"Useless," Max muttered as the four family members arranged themselves around the bottom of his bed, oozing greeting smiles.

"You're looking better, Dad," one of the men said.

"Soon be out of here," the other opined cheerfully.

"We're arranging everything so you'll be properly looked after," one of the women gushed.

The other woman raised her finely arched eyebrows at Christine. "You have someone else to attend to, nurse?" she said dismissively.

"No, she hasn't," Max growled. "I *want* her here, Cynthia. As for looking after me, Prudence—" he glared at the first woman who had spoken "—Sister Delaney is doing a finer job than you'd know how." His eyes stabbed at his elder son. "If I'm looking better, Howard, it's because of her." Then to the younger son. "And you're damned right I'll be soon out of here, Trevor. I've got things to do."

There was an exchange of looks that quickly reached consensus. They proceeded to ignore Christine's presence, as though her existence was far too inconsequential to trouble them in any way. They spoke in turn like a Greek chorus.

"We had a family meeting this weekend, Dad," Howard began.

"We've come to a decision that is in your best interests," Trevor carried on.

"No more stress and strain for you, Max," Prudence chimed in.

"Which put you into hospital in the first place," Howard pointed out.

"You'll be free to enjoy yourself for the rest of your life," Trevor enthused.

"We want you to sign this document," said Cynthia, removing a long envelope from her Gucci handbag, "giving us power of attorney over all your affairs."

Max nodded to himself, his mouth thinning into a grim line before slowly taking on a sardonic curl. "Well, now, the line-up is somewhat unbalanced with four of you to one of me," he drawled. "But I do have Sister Delaney at my side." He looked at Christine with arch emphasis. "It's a fine thing I have a witness to hear what's going on."

"You don't need a witness, Dad," said Howard. "This is all straightforward and aboveboard."

"Yes," the old man growled, then constructed a smile that had all the winsome appeal of a shark's. "I'll be quite happy to sign your document for you in a few weeks' time. But you didn't have to go to this trouble on my behalf. It's all quite unnecessary."

"Why?" Cynthia asked, frowning suspiciously.

"Because I intend to give all my money away. I've already made my decision."

It caught them by surprise.

Prudence was the first to recover. "Well, that truly is in your best interests, Max," she gushed.

"We'll look after it," Howard rushed in. "Manage it properly."

"Make sure you have everything you need, Dad," Trevor supported eagerly. "You can live like a king. No worries."

"Complete peace of mind," Cynthia added, her smile smug with the prospect of having peace of mind herself.

"Yes," Max agreed. His eyes flashed with derisive irony. "But it's not going to you. I'm disposing of it in a different manner. You've had more than enough from me."

In the shocked silence that followed this declaration, Max expounded on his reasons for it. "I've seen the light since I've been in here. You've all led pampered lives. The free ride has to come to an end. It's about time you found out how to earn the money you spend. It'll be the salvation of you as people."

Christine heartily approved these sentiments. But not surprisingly, the Greek chorus spat sheer outrage.

"He's gone mad," said Prudence.

"This is absolute nonsense, Dad," Howard protested.

"You can't sweep everything out from under our feet," Trevor cried.

"What precisely is your idea for disposing of it, Max?" Cynthia bit out, gearing herself to fight tooth and nail for what she wanted.

"I'll be giving it to various worthy organizations and people," Max said calmly, ignoring the others' outbursts. "First on my list is Sister Delaney, who is absolutely essential to not only keeping me alive, but for my general well-being. I'll be paying her five thousand dollars a week to be my personal nurse."

Four pairs of eyes dissected Christine as though she were a loathsome reptile. It instantly stiffened her backbone with resolve. She would side with Max against these people right down the line!

"Dad! That's a quarter of a million dollars a year!" Howard cried, appalled at the prospect of being partially disinherited in favour of a common nurse.

"If it makes me happy, why not?" Max challenged. "From now on I intend to concentrate on doing all the things that make me happy. I've had a warning. I know I can't live forever. So I'm going to make the most of what time I have left, doing whatever I want to do."

There was another exchange of looks between the four at the foot of the bed. It was clear they were facing a personal crisis of enormous proportions. Howard elected himself as first spokesperson.

"We thought when you got rid of Shane you'd come to your senses," he said bitterly. "But you just can't stand losing control, can you?"

"He's gone senile," Cynthia declared.

"Typical of an old man trying to cling to life," Prudence agreed, sneering at Christine. "Sucked in by a pretty face."

"We're not going to take this lying down, Dad," Trevor warned.

"It's no use talking to him," Cynthia declared. "We have to act to protect *our* interests."

Agreement was instant on that point, and they departed in a darkly muttering body.

Christine watched them go with burning resentment in her heart. Shane had not exaggerated their attitude towards him. They *had* wanted to get rid of him. No wonder he wanted to shut the door on his past with those family members. The whole pack of them were self-serving, self-centred vultures, whose one interest was Max's money and their share of it.

She looked at the old man who wanted his grandson back but was too proud to admit his mistakes. His dark eyes were dull and weary. "Wheels within wheels, Sunshine," he said sardonically. "Tell Shane what happened here today. Then make up your own mind where you stand."

"Are you all right, Max?" she asked, automatically feeling for the pulse in his wrist.

He settled back on the pillows and closed his eyes. "Work of the day over," he murmured. "Up to you now."

There was no quickening, not even a flutter in his pulse. He looked worn out but quite serene. Having totally destroyed everyone else's serenity, Christine thought with grim irony, including hers.

She heaved a deep sigh as she left him. Somehow her resolution not to act as a go-between could no longer be sustained. Too many questions had been raised for her to set them aside and ignore what was happening in Shane's family. For some unknown reason, she was not only involved, but playing a more and more central role, whether she wanted to or not.

CHAPTER NINE

No sooner had Christine shut her front door than she heard Shane bounding down the stairs, calling out her name in buoyant anticipation. Despite the questions in her mind, her feet automatically broke into a run. They met in the living room, and Shane whirled her into a wild embrace, arching her body to his to gather another complete imprint of it.

"You feel so good!" he declared with extravagant relish. Then he rained kisses all over her face. "You taste so good. And smell so good..."

She laughingly stilled his head with her hands and he smiled at her, his dark eyes alight with hungry passion. "And I've been waiting all day for you to come home to me," he finished, carrying the fervent words to her lips, then claiming them in a long devouring kiss.

It stirred an urgent and mutual desire. Shane whisked Christine upstairs with him, insisting that he had something to show her, telling her to notice there wasn't a spot of dust anywhere, assuring her the Telecom men had not messed up anything, leading her wickedly and purposefully past the room with the new window and ushering her into the bedroom, which had once been her mother's.

"If you've done anything terrible..." Christine began to threaten, then gasped in amazement at the magnificent four-poster bed that now dominated the room.

"I saw it displayed. Just like that," Shane said, moving up behind her and sliding his arms around her waist to draw her against him. His lips warmly nuzzled her long throat as he murmured, "And I said to myself, that bed is fit for a princess. *My* princess."

"Oh, Shane..." It was all she could manage, overwhelmed by the surge of emotion evoked by his words and his soft kisses and the bed itself.

The four-poster was a wonderfully carved antique, with a canopy of cream lace and drapes of the softest gold silk. Exquisite lace cushions were piled luxuriously against the bedhead, and the gold silk bedspread was beautifully quilted, giving a patterned sheen that was enticingly sensual.

"I could visualise your hair sprayed out on those cushions," Shane said huskily, his hands moving to undo her thick plait. "You and I in a private golden world together, Christine."

How could she not succumb to the magic Shane wove for her? Christine banished any thought that it might be deceptive magic from her mind. This was real, tangible, entrancing, and all her senses were engaged and enthralled by the man who took her into a glorious golden world where loving outshone everything else.

She adored him with her eyes, with her lips, with her body, and basked in the outpouring of adoration from him as they shared once more the wondrous fulfilment of giving themselves completely to each other. If it was only a dream of perfection that could not last indefinitely, Christine was blissfully content to dream in Shane's arms for as long as he was content to hold her. Other concerns held no significance whatsoever.

The ringing of the doorbell was a jarring note in the languorous aftermath of their lovemaking. "Are you expecting anyone?" Shane asked lazily, sliding long tresses of her hair through his fingers.

"No. Are you?" She softly stroked the strong line of his jaw, her eyes smiling into his, ready to accept any other surprises he might spring on her.

"I reserved this time for us," Shane answered, his dark eyes glowing with deep possessiveness. "Let whoever it is go away."

He kissed her, shutting off the outside world with a sensual mastery that Christine was only too happy to accept and encourage. Until she heard someone moving around downstairs. Her heart leapt in agitation at the thought of an intruder breaking into her house.

"Shane!" Her urgent whisper alerted him to the unwelcome noise, as well.

They both tensed, listening with total concentration. A tap was turned on in the kitchen, and water gushed into the sink. A cupboard door was opened and closed. Shane threw Christine a hard questioning look.

She shook her head, denying any possibility of a known visitor.

With lithe purposeful speed, Shane was off the bed and dragging on his jeans while Christine was still paralysed with the shock of what was happening. "Stay here," he hissed.

Despite the danger, Christine felt a thrill of primitive pride as she watched him move to the door, every superbly delineated masculine muscle coiled taut for attack, her warrior intent on defending her home, her man who answered all she wanted in a man.

It was not until he slid out of sight that the thought occurred to her that he might need her support. She quickly scrambled off the bed and started pulling on her clothes, determined on following him as fast as she could. She heard the creak of the stairs under Shane's feet, then a startled cry that sounded distinctly feminine.

"Hold it right there, lady!" Shane commanded in a threatening voice.

"Who are you? What are you doing here?" The shrill panicky questions were followed by a frightened shriek and the sounds of a violent scuffle.

"Be still, you hellcat, or you'll get hurt more than you're bargaining for!" Shane bellowed.

"Help! Rape! Rape!" the woman screamed. "Police! Murder!"

Her voice was abruptly cut off. There was a string of vehement curses from Shane. Then in a more controlled tone he shouted, "It's okay to come down. I've got her."

Christine was already hurtling down the stairs to the living room, imagining that Shane had caught some dangerous drug addict who was desperate to steal something to sell for a fix. She skidded to a halt in the kitchen doorway, shocked at the bleeding scratches that were clawed down Shane's arm.

He had the intruder cornered between the pantry cupboard and the sink. It took Christine several seconds for recognition of the wild-eyed woman to dawn on her. It was the short mop of curly red hair that registered first. Then the distinctive snub nose and pixie ears.

"Sandra!" she cried in horrified surprise. "What are you doing here?"

"You know this woman?" Shane demanded, looking distinctly put out by the thought.

"Yes. Sandra Allsop. But she's supposed to be in Melbourne."

"So what the hell is she doing sneaking into your home?"

"I don't know. I don't know how she got here or why. Let her go and we'll find out."

"Thief!" Shane muttered, eyeing Sandra suspiciously as he reluctantly eased his body away from her.

"All brawn and no brain," Sandra spat at him as soon as she was released. "Airhead!"

"Make one wrong move," Shane snarled, "and I'll clip those bloody claws of yours to the quick."

"Men like you need gelding."

"Maiming gives you your kicks, does it?" Shane fired with towering contempt.

"Stop it! Both of you!" Christine cut in strongly.

She succeeded in drawing their attention away from each other long enough for her to strike a note of calm sanity. "What are you doing here, Sandra? What happened to the commission to restore paintings in Melbourne?"

"Disaster! It was all a disaster!" she cried, throwing up her hands in despair.

"What was?"

"The business was a front for selling fakes. They're all in jail. And I've had days of grilling by the police before they'd believe in my innocence. I can't get my belongings back. Everything's been impounded. I'm stony broke with nowhere to go, so I hitchhiked from Melbourne, and if you can't help me, Christine, I'm in big trouble."

"Of course I'll help."

"She was about to help herself, if you ask me," Shane muttered grimly. "Don't forget she broke into your house, Christine."

"I did not!" Sandra snapped at him. "I had a spare key from when I lived here before. When Christine didn't answer the doorbell, I knew she wouldn't mind if I came inside to wait for her."

"That's true, Shane," Christine assured him. "Sandra rented the upstairs rooms for six months before she left for Melbourne."

"Who is this guy, anyway?" Sandra demanded. "What's he doing here?"

"This is Shane Courtney. My, uh . . ."

"Lover," Shane supplied in no uncertain terms, moving over to curl a possessive arm around Christine's shoulders.

A wild confusion of expressions flitted over Sandra's face as she stared goggle-eyed at the evidence in front of her. Shane, clad only in jeans. Christine barefooted, bare-legged, her nurse's uniform slightly awry and her hair in total disarray. Christine felt her cheeks start to burn as she saw the embarrassed flush sweep into Sandra's.

"Well, I hope he's got more between his legs than he's got between his ears," came the waspish comment.

"Sandra!" Christine protested. "It's not like that."

"Who do you think you're kidding, Christine? I don't blame you for taking on such a handsome hunk, but he certainly wasn't on the scene a week ago. And if you ask me, he's downright dangerous. The way he manhandled me—"

"Shane is living here, Sandra," Christine put in with quiet dignity. "He was simply protecting me and my property. And I happen to think he's well equipped in every department."

"Thank you, my princess," Shane said smugly, dropping a kiss on her hair.

"Living here!" Appalled dismay was written all over Sandra's face.

Christine nodded. "Shane is now renting the up-stairs rooms."

"Oh, no!" Sandra wailed. "Then there's no room for me."

"I'm afraid they are all taken."

"There is a solution," Shane slid in, drawing their attention to him. He smiled at Christine, his eyes gleaming with triumphantly wicked purpose. "You can't turn away a destitute friend. Rent your room to Sandra and move upstairs with me."

"You're absolutely right, Christine," Sandra put in eagerly. "He is well equipped between his ears. Not an airhead at all."

Christine could not deny it was a ready solution to Sandra's problem, yet Shane's quick opportunism stirred an odd prickle of disquiet. She suddenly re-membered Max's argument that nothing happened by chance with Shane, and that she was a part of a planned powerplay that Max was trying to neutralise.

She wished she hadn't let Shane distract her from taking up that particular issue with him. She wasn't certain in her own mind how he would react to Max's latest manoeuvres. All she really knew was that Shane had been trying to manoeuvre her upstairs with him from the moment he had set foot inside her home, and now he was grasping a quick and certain way to suc-ceed.

Her hesitation over his suggestion earned a chal-lenging frown from him and a rush of agitated misery from her friend.

"I've messed this up, haven't I? You don't want me intruding on your privacy. Besides, I haven't got the means to pay rent at the moment. I'd better get out of here and leave you to it."

"I'll pay your rent," Shane offered.

Sandra looked her astonishment. "Why on earth should you do that?"

"That's enough, Shane," Christine said decisively. Neither he nor his grandfather was going to buy her for any purpose! "Sandra, we'll work something out between us, but first I want to speak to Shane alone. You must be hungry. Help yourself to anything in the kitchen and I'll be back to talk it over with you later. Okay?"

Relief flooded Sandra's face. "Thanks, Christine. I knew I could rely on you."

Christine's responding smile held a touch of irony. She might very well need Sandra's sympathetic support if her dream with Shane came to a shattering end. She turned to the man who had declared himself her lover and dragged in a deep breath.

"Let's go upstairs."

His smile held satisfaction. "Saves double tripping if we take some of your things on the way."

"I'll help," said Sandra eagerly.

Christine sighed, realising she was hoisted on her own petard, since she had well and truly accepted Shane as her lover. She might as well move upstairs with him, at least until some other resolution to their affair presented itself to her. Shane Courtney was, af-

ter all, her perfect man, and he had not proved anything less so far. She pushed aside the doubts Max had
seeded, and gave in to the inevitable. Until further notice.

Shane and Sandra were cheerfully cooperative as
they helped Christine move the practical substance of
her daily necessities upstairs. Sandra even went so far
as to fuss over the injury she had done to Shane, insisting on cleaning up the scratches and dabbing on
antiseptic cream. Suddenly the two antagonists were
the best of friends, silkily courteous to each other,
arousing Christine's deepest suspicions about their
complicity.

"I wouldn't put it past you to have planned all this,
Shane Courtney," she muttered to him on their final
trip to his bedroom.

He grinned at her. "I would have if I'd known."

"Anything to get your own way."

"With you, yes."

"Totally ruthless."

"Ruthlessly devoted to the pursuit of our happiness."

Christine couldn't find a riposte to that. It made her
feel ridiculously happy. Nevertheless, she was not
about to let Shane distract her from other important
issues. She finished putting the last of her things in the
huge old wardrobe that had once been her mother's,
then swung around to face him.

He was propped up on the pillows of the four-poster bed, intently studying the framed photograph of her mother she had placed on the bedside table.

"That was taken when my mother was the same age as I am now," Christine informed him.

He shook his head. "I feel I've seen that face somewhere before." He looked at Christine, searching for similarities that would account for his feeling.

"My eyes are the same shape," she said helpfully.

He smiled. "Your eyes are uniquely yours, Christine. It must be some weird sense of deja vu. Or maybe your mother's face fits the image you've drawn of her for me."

Christine briefly wondered what her mother would have thought of the changes Shane had made to her house. But the past was the past. It was the future that concerned her now.

"About our happiness, Shane," Christine began determinedly. "I think you ought to know what your grandfather's been up to."

One eyebrow lifted in disdain. "It doesn't make any difference to me what he's been up to."

"He offered me five thousand dollars a week to be his private personal nurse."

Shane jerked upright, surprised out of his supposedly bored disinterest. His forehead slowly creased in puzzlement. "Why? For what purpose?"

Christine shrugged. "He said he could outbid you any day."

"But he's never been personally vindictive in all his life. Why is he starting now?" Shane shook his head. "It doesn't make sense."

"Well, there's more. He told me to tell you."

"He was that explicit?"

"Yes."

She related the family meeting that had taken place around Max's bed, word for word as much as she could remember. Shane listened with guarded interest, a sardonic smile playing over his lips as she described the family's reactions to Max's shocking announcements.

"This goes far deeper than I thought," Shane mused. "He's thrown down the gauntlet. He's started a war. He's attacking everyone. And there's only one thing we can be certain of."

"What's that?" asked Christine.

"He intends to win."

"I think he really wants you to go to him, Shane."

"That will be the last thing I'll ever do."

"He's an old man..."

"In full possession of his faculties."

"What's going to happen? What does he want to win?"

"I don't know," said Shane slowly. There was a touch of wry appreciation in his tone as he added, "But I expect from here on in, life will suddenly be full of little surprises."

"What if he truly means to give it all away?" Christine questioned, wanting Shane's reaction to that.

"It's his money. It's his choice."

"You don't care if it goes to whatever worthy causes he chooses?"

"Not one bit."

Unforgiving... tough as nails... stubborn young buck... Max's words ran through Christine's mind as she observed the steely pride on Shane's face.

"Your parents weren't there today, were they?" she softly probed.

"No."

"Well, where are they?"

"In heaven, according to my grandfather. In hell, according to dear Aunt Cynthia and the others."

"They're dead."

"Yes. They died before I ever knew them."

Christine felt a surge of relief at this information. It had seemed so unnatural to her that his mother and father should want to get rid of him. "So who brought you up?" she asked.

"My grandfather appointed Cynthia and Howard my caretakers for when he didn't have time for me."

"Did he have much time for you?"

"More than for his other grandchildren. Which still wasn't much until I grew old enough to be of useful interest to him. According to Cynthia, I was the son of the favourite son. For which she heartily hated me."

That threw considerable light on Shane's dark background. The four Courtneys Christine had met today would certainly band together to get rid of any threat to their inheritance. A favourite would be anathema to them, particularly a favourite who had disassociated himself from them.

"Didn't your grandfather realise that you were unhappy with Cynthia and Howard?" she asked softly.

Shane's grimace was full of irony. "They always put on a show of caring in front of my grandfather, and he didn't want to know any different. Looking back now, I think he was devastated by the loss of my father, who was the only one of his sons in the same mould as himself. Howard and Trevor were younger, and either they couldn't compete or didn't want to. Anyhow, with my father gone and with the other two uninterested in the business world, my grandfather more or less shut himself off from the rest of us."

Until Shane showed promise of being like his father, Christine thought. Was it the unloving negligence throughout his childhood that Shane couldn't forget or forgive? Yet how could his involvement with her be a payback for that?

"I'm sorry, Shane," she murmured sympathetically, but he didn't hear her.

His expression reflected a dark inner world of bitter memories. The need to question him further was swept aside by a strong impulse to take him in her arms and promise him, give him, all the love he had never known, obliterating the cold loneliness of his past with the warmth and comfort and security of true caring.

Christine was momentarily stunned by the depth of her feeling for him. It bore no relation to the dizzy pleasure of being in love, and it went beyond natural human sympathy. The tug on her soul had a frightening intensity, giving her a sense of vulnerability that she had never known before. If she was wrong about Shane, if he was deceiving her about his feelings for her, using her for some ulterior purpose...

"Shane..." Her cry of need emerged as little more than a husky plea.

His eyes instantly focussed on hers. "That's all water under the bridge, Christine," he said dismissively. "I've made my own life, and I couldn't care less what any of them thinks or does now."

Except for his grandfather, Christine silently amended. His pride insisted he didn't care, but he did. Christine was certain of it. The bond between them was not broken, but the barriers of pride were still very much in place.

Her need for the truth was even more urgent now. Was she the tool to break those barriers? Could she do that with love, or was she only a weapon of some sort to swing the balance of power?

"What do you want me to do, Shane?" she asked. "Your grandfather has offered me a quarter of a million dollars a year."

"Refuse it," he commanded categorically.

Christine's spine stiffened. Shane might call his grandfather the General, but he was beginning to sound quite the dictator himself. He needed a good jolt, from her point of view.

"With all your wealth, Shane Courtney, that's very easy for you to say. When you're as poor as I am, such a sum of money looks very attractive."

He looked startled. Then a glitter of steely resolution swept into his eyes. "The solution is simple. Tell my grandfather you're going to marry me. He'll find that offer hard to outbid."

Christine felt a cold frisson of shock at the sheer ruthlessness of what could only be a shut-out manoeuvre on his grandfather. Shane was not thinking of her at all. Not what she felt. Nor what kind of future they might have together.

"I will not tell him any such thing," she said, sickened by the lack of caring in his proposal. "You can't be serious," she added, pleading for some emotional reassurance from him.

"Oh, yes, I am!" He sprang off the bed like a predatory animal, a pouncing gleam in his eyes. "So that takes care of your future," he said triumphantly. "It's with me."

"I haven't said yes."

He swung her off her feet, carried her to the bed, pinned her down and tried to use his mouth to ravishing advantage. Christine stubbornly kept evading his marauding lips. She was not about to let him drug her senses into compliance with some predetermined purpose. Not this time. Nor ever again. No matter what she felt for him.

"Tell me—" she gasped.

"Say yes."

"—what happened—"

"Say yes, Christine."

"—between you—"

"You have to say yes."

"—and your grandfather."

He groaned. "Let's keep him out of this."

"It's because of him you asked me to marry you."

"I *want* to marry you. And I'm going to."

"I won't agree until you tell me why all this is going on."

He gave a hiss of exasperation. "The same reason for what happened before. My grandfather wants to give me the title but still hold the reins of power. I will not accept a position where he has any veto over the decisions I make."

Christine looked at him in astonishment. "And that's all this is about?"

"We are talking about a billion-dollar business empire," he informed her dryly.

"Oh!" she said.

"Now say yes."

"And you truly don't care if he gives it away?"

He sighed heavily. "Christine, from what you've told me, the General simply wants a good war to liven up what's left of his life. I will not take part in a fight over the spoils. If he thinks dragging you into it will force my hand on that score, he can think again."

"Ah!" said Christine with grim satisfaction. "I'm starting to see how your mind works, Shane Courtney."

"Then you'll know that I desperately want you to say yes."

Her mind swiftly clicked through everything she knew, fitting it together as best she could. Maybe she had been the perfect gauntlet for Shane to throw down to his grandfather. No more veto in his personal life! Marriage to a socially unsuitable woman would certainly ram that home beyond recall, as well as serve the purpose of thumbing his nose at the rest of his family.

"The answer is no," she said unequivocally.

"Why?" He looked taken aback.

"Firstly, because it was a spur of the moment decision, which had to do with winning your war with your grandfather. And not with me."

"I've thought of nothing but you since we met," he defended stoutly.

"Secondly, you didn't ask me properly."

"I can rectify that," he insisted.

"And thirdly, since I've now become the bone you're fighting over, I'm interested to see how far your grandfather will go to outbid you, Shane."

He looked totally shocked. "How can he give you a better counterproposal?"

"He might offer to marry me himself," she replied blandly, determined to teach Shane that she didn't appreciate his pragmatic way of arranging her life for her. If he didn't truly love her, if this proposal was only a bid for control, no way would she ever marry him.

His shock turned to horror. "He's seventy-five, Christine!"

"And a very interesting personality."

"You can't be serious!"

"He likes me. He calls me his sunshine."

A deep growl emanated from Shane's throat. "I call you my princess."

Max's words flitted through her mind. *Tell Shane what happened here today. Then make up your mind where you stand.* Shane's eyes were burning with a fierce possessiveness. Maybe it wasn't only about winning. She hated the way he had leapt to a proposal to counter his grandfather's proposition, yet she could not dismiss the memory of what they had shared in this bed earlier this afternoon, and the way Shane had treated her like his princess.

"That's very nice, Shane," she conceded, and wound her arms around his neck. "You're very attractive. But I can't seriously consider your proposal. I do need to find out what your grandfather is going to say to all this."

She was beginning to think like a Courtney. And speak like one. "For the moment," she continued, "and it was what you wanted before, I'll just have you as my upstairs lover."

After all, she didn't want to completely give up on the chance that Shane was genuine in his feeling for her. But she was not about to be rushed into any decision under such dubious circumstances.

CHAPTER TEN

CHRISTINE BARELY NOTICED her walk to the hospital the next morning. Her mind was buzzing. The day ahead of her pulsed with possibilities she could never have dreamed of a week ago.

Of course, she had no intention whatsoever of accepting Max's offer to be his personal private nurse. But she was going to tell him about Shane's offer of marriage. That should provoke Max into revealing what he meant about her being used as a payback for the past. Christine wanted that cleared up before she seriously considered marrying Shane.

Which she wanted to do.

Very much.

If he truly loved her and wanted her with him for the rest of eternity, as he had declared very convincingly last night.

However, she had only known him four days, and eternity was somewhat longer. Impulsive wartime marriages didn't usually last that long. Particularly when there was a general intent on winning his way. Which was not Shane's way.

A quickly settled peace was what Christine needed. Which meant she had to remain a diplomatic go-between. Only then would she be able to gauge if a future with Shane was definitely in the cards, and he wasn't playing some sleight of hand with her to gain some advantage over his grandfather.

Christine arrived at the vascular ward in a glow of optimistic anticipation, only to have that dashed by the first surprise of the day. Max Courtney no longer occupied bed nine. He had signed himself out of the hospital. The General was on the loose to wage war however he saw fit.

The night staff reported that nothing and no-one could talk him out of his decision to go. He had been totally intransigent in insisting he could take care of his own health. He had signed a responsibility disclaimer, walked out of the hospital at ten o'clock last night, climbed into a taxi, and that was the last anyone had seen or heard of him.

Christine pondered this new development as she went about her morning routine. Had Max's offer to her yesterday been a short-term tactic to stir dissension between her and Shane? He had certainly used it to flout his family's plans for him, yet he had not waited for her answer. Which meant he could not have been serious about it. Or he had failed to provoke the result he wanted from it.

Christine concentrated on thinking like a Courtney. She soon figured out what had happened. Max had not gone until after visiting hours at the hospital were well and truly over last night. He had waited to see if Shane would come, spurred to battle on her behalf. When that had not happened, Max had decided some other tactic was needed to bring Shane to heel.

Although going home did not seem to be a strong move. Medically speaking it was not a wise move, either. Christine could not help worrying about that. She did not want Shane's grandfather to suffer another heart attack. Apart from feeling a growing fondness for the old warrior, it would be terrible for him to die before he and Shane were reconciled.

Perhaps that was sentimentality on her part. Men were such a different breed to women. Perhaps they really enjoyed war, pitting their strengths and sharpening their wits against each other. For all she knew, they probably found peace hopelessly dull.

In any event, it was not a dull morning at the hospital. Soon after ten o'clock, Cynthia and Howard Courtney arrived with two psychiatrists in tow, and created a tremendous row when they were told that Max had flown the coop, so to speak. Of course, the ward sister didn't put it that way, but Cynthia and Howard definitely saw it in those terms.

"How could you let a sick, senile old man simply walk out?" Cynthia screeched.

"He can't be held responsible for himself!" Howard cried accusingly.

And so on and so on at ever rising decibels.

It was quickly established that Max had not gone home. Christine was called in and grilled as to his whereabouts, since she was supposed to have been hired as his private and personal nurse. She could offer no help in their quest to find him, although it was clear that she was not believed.

"We'll sue the hospital for this," Cynthia threatened. "You've let a madman loose. God knows what he'll do next."

"Appalling administration!" Howard ranted.

The ward sister sternly proclaimed that Max Courtney was in full possession of his faculties and had every right to refuse treatment and direct his life as he saw fit. The form he had signed relieved the hospital of all responsiblity for his decision.

The psychiatrists looked discomfited.

Christine could barely restrain a smile.

The General had obviously anticipated this move from his family and was undoubtedly a good few steps ahead of them. They left on a bitter note of defeat, still hurling undeserved invectives at the staff.

Where was Max?

And what was he up to?

Those questions were not only on the Courtney family's minds, but also on Christine's. As soon as her lunchbreak came she telephoned Shane to let him know this latest development. His response was totally noncommittal. Christine put the telephone receiver down with a frustrated sigh. Apparently a stand-off was a stand-off, and that was that.

She had completely forgotten about what Shane had planned for today, until her shift ended and Sandra met her outside the hospital.

"I know it's none of my business, Christine," she started, her whole expression determined on making it her business. "But your lover seems to be taking a lot upon himself. Particularly with your house."

She suddenly remembered the patched-up wall around the new window. "It's okay, Sandra. I know about the painters."

"What about the architect? And the carpet?" Sandra said. "Do you know about them?"

"What carpet?"

"The new green one for upstairs. Someone came to measure the rooms this morning and it was laid this afternoon."

Christine laughed. Max was not the only one who was full of surprises. Shane had his own polished style in that department.

"How can you laugh?" Sandra protested. "That man is dangerous."

"Dangerous? I thought you'd become the best of friends," Christine teased.

"I think he's a takeover expert," Sandra declared with brooding suspicion. "He's taken you over, and now he's taking over your house. He can claim half of it, you know, if you let him live there for a year as your lover. Then there goes your security. Christine, you've got to be very careful with de facto relationships."

"I don't think I need to worry about that with Shane," Christine said with a confident smile.

"You're besotted with him," Sandra accused, then tempered it with a rueful smile. "Not that I can blame you. He's one hell of a hunk. Smart, too. But it does pay to be wary in these uncertain times."

"I agree," Christine soothed.

"There's something very fishy about the way Shane Courtney gets things done. It's too fast, if you know what I mean."

"I think money has something to do with it," Christine said dryly.

"And just where does his money come from?" Sandra asked with arch suspicion. "If you ask me, he's got some very questionable connections, Christine."

"Like what?"

"I don't know. But he got the police in Melbourne to release all my stuff this morning. They wouldn't do it for me, but they did it for him. No trouble at all. And everything delivered to me by express courier. Now, I'm not saying I'm not grateful, Christine—"

"Shane is very kind and thoughtful," she popped in, delighted that he had gone out of his way to help her friend.

"—but things don't happen like that for ordinary people like you and me," Sandra finished, her hands eloquently dramatising the point.

"I expect Shane put a lawyer onto the problem," Christine said matter-of-factly.

"And who uses lawyers most?" Sandra pounced. "Crooks! That's who! Crooks and con-men!"

Christine sighed. "Sandra, I know you've just been through a horrible experience, and I can understand that your view has been coloured by it—"

"Too right, it has! You've got to look before you leap, Christine," her friend retorted with feeling.

"I promise I'm doing that," Christine assured her.

Sandra wagged a finger. "It's just as well you've got me in the house. I'm your independent witness if things go wrong."

"I appreciate that, Sandra. Life is full of surprises and it's always good to have a witness."

"Right! I'm glad you can see that much," Sandra said with considerable relief.

"Is Shane at home with the architect now?" Christine asked, wondering what plans he had for more alterations to her house.

"No. The architect was there this morning. And Shane went out this afternoon, leaving me to supervise the carpet layers. As soon as they left, I locked up and whizzed down here to catch you before *he* got home and put stars in your eyes again."

Christine smiled. "Thanks, Sandra. I know you have my best interests at heart."

"You can rely on me to look out for them," Sandra said gravely. "And now that I've got my things back, I'll go around to the galleries tomorrow and see if I can get some work. I won't keep you waiting long for rent money, Christine."

"Don't worry about it. I'm glad that all your belongings have been recovered."

They turned the corner into Christine's cul-de-sac and Sandra frowned over her shoulder. "That guy is still there in the blue car. He was watching us, Christine. Now he's shoved a newspaper in front of his face."

Christine glanced around, then shook her head at her friend. "So what, Sandra? Is it a crime for a guy to look at two young women passing by?"

"He was there before. When I went to meet you."

"Maybe he's waiting for someone."

"Maybe he's watching who comes in and out of our lane."

"Sandra!" Christine rolled her eyes. "That's getting really paranoid."

"Okay. I'll shut up. But I can't help feeling something very funny's going on around here since you took Shane Courtney into your life."

Christine thought it was more a case of Shane having taken her into his life, but since that would only reinforce Sandra's view of him as a takeover expert, she said nothing.

Shane was home when they arrived. He showed no sign of being concerned about anything. He was brimming with good humour, not even chastising Sandra for giving away his surprise about the green carpet, which was so wonderfully thick and soft that Christine had to take off her shoes to feel it with her bare feet.

"This is heavenly, Shane. But I think I ought to point out you're investing a lot of money in my house."

"Just proving that I care about your comfort." He drew her into his arms. "Showing you what it will be like when you're married to me."

"I haven't said yes yet." Her eyes flashed a hard warning. "And you're wasting both your time and money if you think you can buy my consent."

He winced. "Forget what I said about outbidding my grandfather, Christine. It was an unconsidered reaction to—" his eyes darkened with old memories "—to past experience with the lure of wealth." Then he smiled and softly stroked her cheek. "I know you're not like that. I knew from the beginning, when you wouldn't let me buy you cherries."

Again she felt the strong tug on her soul, and when Shane kissed her, Christine met him more than halfway, her defences overwhelmed by a surge of love and compassion. Had everything in Shane's life been tainted and twisted by his grandfather's wealth? Had she herself triggered his fierce reaction last night by saying Max's offer was attractive to someone as poor as herself? What was behind all that was happening she did not know, but at least she could give her love freely. There was no price on that.

"You will say yes," Shane said with complete confidence, still tasting her response to him.

Christine instinctively shied away from the issue of marriage. She wanted to be absolutely sure of Shane's love first. If that was true and steadfast, time would not change it. Nor would any interference from Max.

"What about the architect?" she asked, drawing back to see the expression in Shane's eyes.

They shone with happy anticipation. "Drawing up plans for the future."

"You're not to go ahead with them unless I approve."

"Definitely a togetherness project," he promised.

Christine found togetherness with Shane a very exciting concept. She struggled to resist it for a while. "What about your grandfather? Aren't you the least bit worried about him?"

Shane frowned at her persistent concern on that subject. "Adopting guerilla warfare. Attack and retreat. Regrouping for another onslaught," he answered dismissively.

"But he didn't go home."

"Of course not. The family would be waiting for him there."

"He might need help, Shane."

"Nonsense! He knows perfectly well what he's doing. Forget my grandfather and concentrate on me."

"It was because of your grandfather you asked me to marry you," she reminded him.

"No," he denied forcefully. "It was the threat he posed, Christine. I couldn't bear the thought of him coming between us."

She searched his eyes, desperately wanting to believe him.

"When you find what you've been looking for all your life, and you have it within your grasp, you don't let someone take it away from you, Christine. You do whatever has to be done to hold on to it," Shane explained in a voice that throbbed with a thousand unfulfilled needs.

Christine was silenced by it, humbled by it, and could only hope she *was* what Shane had been looking for all his life, and it wasn't a dream that would disintegrate under the pressures of real life.

Her gaze fell on the photograph of her mother on the bedside table. Rose Delaney had been shut out by the people who should have cared for her at the time of her greatest need, yet she had spent her life answering the needs of others and had imbued her daughter with the same sense of caring. Was it the giving and the sharing that Shane yearned for and had found with her? Shut out by his family, pride driving him to show his grandfather he could be successful without the old man's backing... Had Shane ever experienced this kind of loving with anyone else?

Whatever the reason, his resolve to marry her certainly didn't weaken over the next two days. He obviously considered that her consent was only a matter of committed persistence on his part.

On Thursday, an impressive array of office equipment was installed in the back bedroom upstairs. Sandra did some muttering about the blue car having been changed to a grey one, the watchers working in shifts. Christine floated along on the relentless tide of Shane's courtship, waiting for the future to resolve itself.

On Friday, Shane met her as she came off her shift at the hospital and took her into the city to look at engagement rings. He fancied an emerald with diamonds. Christine refused to indicate any preference at all. Shane insisted that the third finger on her left hand be measured. A look of mutual understanding passed between him and the jeweller.

They had a fine relaxing dinner on the open terrace section of The Phantom of The Opera restaurant at Campbell's Cove. They sat directly across from the opera house, idly watching the commuter ferries churning in and out of Circular Quay. It was a soft, balmy evening, made for romance, and Christine was very close to succumbing to the commitment Shane wanted from her.

"What would your life be like if you did take over from your grandfather, Shane?" she asked, wondering precisely what she would be taking on if she married him. "I mean, wouldn't running such a huge business take up all your time?"

"Unlike my grandfather, I know how to delegate, Christine. And I already have a trusted team of people trained to take on what I require of them." He paused, then quietly added, "I have no intention of neglecting my wife or family. Having found the woman I want to share my life with, I shall share it with her."

She flushed with tingling pleasure and turned her gaze out over the harbour. "You said family. Do you want children, Shane?"

"Do you?"

"Someday."

"Then we'll have them someday."

"I didn't say I'd marry you. I don't even know how you feel about having a wife with a career of her own."

"I believe every person has the right to fulfil whatever they want to do in life. I'd say to my wife...go for it!"

She swung her gaze sharply to his. "What if it conflicted with what you wanted to do?"

He smiled. "I'm a problem solver."

Christine took a deep breath. "What if you don't get your grandfather's business?"

Shane's smile did not falter. "I'm still a problem solver. And a highly successful one, I might add." He reached across the table and took her hand, enfolding it in his, gently caressing it. His dark eyes captured hers with deep intensity. "You will never want for anything with me, Christine."

Her heart fluttered a fervent yes. She almost said it then and there. She didn't know what held her back. Shane was so strong and steady and resolute, totally fair in his thinking, and so generous in his giving, what more could she possibly want from him? He was everything she could ever want in a man. The perfect lover. The perfect partner for life. It had to be right. The feeling that flowed from him had to be true. And her feeling for him made her want to give him everything he had missed out on. Did time matter when no more proof of loving was needed?

"Let's go home," she said before temptation got the better of good judgement.

She did not have to hurry into a decision. It could wait until Max surfaced again and cleared up the situation. She had no doubt that the General would make another foray into her life, and no doubt that Shane would remain at her side until he did. The final reckoning of what was real or not could then be made.

They caught a taxi home. Christine noticed the blue car parked near the corner when they turned into the cul-de-sac, but there was no-one in it. Sandra was definitely neurotic about watchers. Her experience in Melbourne must have left her with some kind of persecution complex, Christine decided.

The question marks about Sandra's state of mind were raised again a few moments later. Christine and Shane were still alighting from the taxi when Sandra flew out of the house, leaving the front door wide open.

"That's it!" she cried, throwing her hands up in the air and gesticulating wildly. "I told you that you were being taken over, Christine. Now it's time you dealt with it. And be firm about it, too. You let me have your room and I'm not going to be kicked out for anyone."

"Sandra! Calm down! No-one's kicking you out," Christine assured her.

"Yes, they are!" She stabbed an accusing finger at Shane. "And it's all his doing! He was plotting it all along. But I will not be bought off. I'm Christine's friend and I'm standing by her, Shane Courtney."

"For heaven's sake, Sandra! What are you talking about?" Christine pleaded.

"Look at this!" She shook a fistful of hundred-dollar notes at both of them. "A thousand dollars for me to move out. What kind of honest money is that? They've got to be crooks, Christine.''

"Who is *they*, Sandra?''

"Him.'' She glared at Shane, then pointed at the house. ''And the old codger in there who reckons he's his grandfather.''

"Max Courtney?'' Christine asked sharply.

"That's the name he gave. I thought he'd only come to visit. But once he was inside, he had the gall to say you were his private and personal nurse, Christine. And that he'd come for you to look after him. Said he was paying you five thousand dollars a week. And he'd be needing my room.''

"Bold move,'' Shane murmured appreciatively. "But what's he after?''

"Let's find out,'' said Christine.

Sandra looked at the thousand dollars in her hand. "There's big trouble in this,'' she muttered, then flounced away from them, tramping towards the path under the trees that led to Oxford Street.

"Sandra! Where are you going?'' Christine called.

"I'll come back when they're gone!'' she flung over her shoulder and kept right on tramping.

Christine and Shane looked at each other, shrugged, then turned towards the front door. With a firm and purposeful step, Christine led the way into the house, Shane closing the door behind them.

Max was seated at the head of the table in the living room. He looked every inch the General in command, resplendent in a three-piece suit, one hand resting on a silver-tipped walking cane, the other toying with the largest of Havana cigars. On the table was a silver flask, the kind that held brandy or whisky. The glass beside the flask indicated how he had been passing the time.

"Max Courtney! You know you're not supposed to be smoking. And you shouldn't be drinking, either," Christine scolded.

Max lifted the cigar to his lips and puffed away as though it was the sweetest nectar of life.

"Hello, Grandfather," Shane said, moving past Christine to the foot of the table. "Come to say you're sorry?"

Max watched the smoke rise, pointedly ignoring both Shane's words and his presence. His gaze wandered around the room until he decided to smile at Christine.

"Nice home, Sunshine," he said. "Needs a bit of refurbishment. I'll bring in an architect and an interior decorator tomorrow. I'm really going to enjoy staying here."

CHAPTER ELEVEN

INTENSE PROVOCATION. There was not going to be any retreat from this battlefield. It was make or break time for all of them.

The thoughts flitted through Christine's mind as she strode forward. Tactful diplomacy was out, she decided, and face-to-face confrontation was the order of the day.

She snatched the smoking cigar from between Max's fingers, turned it into a soggy mess by jamming it into his drink, whipped the glass and the flask off the table and was on her way to the garbage bin in the kitchen before he could react.

"Sunshine! Where's your humanity?" he cried in protest. "We're not in hospital now."

"How did you find out where I lived?" she asked, punctuating the question with a satisfactory bang of the garbage lid.

"I bribed the ward sister for your address. She was a hard negotiator. Cost me a hundred dollars."

Christine stalked into the living room, breathing fire. "Well, Shane did better. It only cost him thirty dollars."

"Hmph," said Max. "Must have been dealing with a simpleton."

"Gino is not a simpleton. His Italian soul simply can't resist romance."

Max grimaced. "You've been deluded, Sunshine. There's no romance here." He nodded to the foot of the table where Shane sat in stony silence. "I've come to rescue you from him."

"I don't need rescuing," Christine retorted. "And I'm not going to be your private nurse, either."

"I've come prepared for that." He drew what was obviously a cheque from his inner coat pocket and held it out to her with an air of bland confidence.

Christine took it, drew out a chair, sat down, picked up the silver lighter he had left on the table after lighting his cigar, then proceeded to put the cheque over the flame.

"That's a quarter of a million dollars!" Max cried in horror.

"As you said yourself, Max, compromise is a word used by the devil. Let it burn!"

"Are you bargaining for more money, Sunshine?"

She dropped the charred paper into the ashtray and looked him straight in the eye. "You know what your problem is, Max? You've been ruined by your wealth."

He laughed at the idea.

"You think it can buy you anything, and you can't stand to admit you're wrong when it doesn't," Christine continued. "I think it's a good idea for you to give it all away. It might be the making of you as a person."

He stopped laughing and eyed her with an oddly soft look. "Someone else once said that to me."

"Then it's a pity you didn't listen, because it's well past time you did, Max. I want you to get this straight. No more offers. No more bids."

"I could make you a rich woman," he persisted.

"I don't care! That's not important to me!"

Max relaxed in his chair, an ironic little smile quirking his lips. "How the past repeats itself!"

Shane gave a mirthless laugh. "Got it wrong again, didn't you, Grandfather? You're now faced with two of us who can't be bought."

Max ignored Shane's sardonic remark. His dark eyes surveyed Christine with new respect. "I had to find out," he said quietly.

Christine didn't know what past Max was referring to, and she was sick to death of him talking in riddles, implying things instead of spelling them out. "Well," she said in exasperation. "There are a few things *I* want to find out, Max."

"What do you want to know, Sunshine?" he said with warm indulgence.

"Why did you make that ridiculous offer to me in the first place?"

His expression underwent an immediate change. He glared down the table at his grandson. "To spike his guns. If he hadn't brought you into it, I would have given him everything."

"You brought Christine into it, not me, Grandfather," Shane retorted, glaring right back at the old man. "Trying to lure her into your camp to make me follow."

Max thumped his fist on the table. "You shouldn't have used her."

Shane thumped even harder. "I'm not using her!" he shouted. "I would never use Christine." He leant forward, his whole body glowering with fierce intent. "No matter what you say or do, Grandfather, I'm going to marry her. And to hell with you giving me anything!"

"Hold it right there!" Christine commanded. "I haven't said I'll marry you, Shane. And I want to know why your grandfather thinks you were using me."

The old man relaxed into his chair, shaking his head. "Marriage! Well, that certainly puts a different complexion on things," he muttered.

"I haven't said yes yet," Christine stated, determined to remain neutral until she'd heard everything she wanted to hear.

"Why not?" Max looked put out. He frowned at his grandson. "What's wrong with him? Too much like me? You'd better start changing, Shane. Don't make the same mistake I did."

"What mistake was that?" Christine asked, feeling bewildered by the sudden about-face. Did marriage make everything right? Was Max a strict moralist who didn't approve of two consenting adults living together?

His face suddenly became guarded. "Never you mind about what happened with me, Sunshine. I was too old to change my ways. So I didn't get what I wanted."

"Which was?" Christine persisted.

"The woman I loved," he answered gruffly.

"*You* loved someone?" Shane asked incredulously.

Max looked startled. "You didn't know?"

"How would I know?" Shane demanded. "What did you ever show me of your private life? I was the kid you handed over to Cynthia, remember? The one sent off to boarding school for six years. The one you finished up ordering out of your life because I wouldn't become a yes-man to your every whim and fancy."

"I handed you over to Cynthia because I thought you'd benefit from a woman's touch," Max stoutly defended. "And that school was good for you. Gave you self-discipline. And I didn't want a yes-man. I wanted some respect from you."

He glowered at Shane. "Telling me how to run things as though I didn't know." He leaned forward aggressively and tapped the table with his finger. "Who made that company what it is? Who?"

"You did, Grandfather," Shane acknowledged mockingly. "And because you wouldn't take the initiatives I suggested, it's been sliding downhill for the last eight years."

"Didn't have anything left to work for, did I?" the old man countered. "No-one to pass it on to. I had to have a heart attack before you'd come back to me."

"You told me to go," Shane grimly reminded him.

"You should've given me time to get used to your ideas," Max growled. "Old dogs can't learn new tricks in a day."

"You wouldn't listen."

"You wanted it all your own way. No respect."

They glared at each other.

"Why don't you both say you're sorry?" Christine suggested quietly.

A stubborn silence reigned.

It was broken by a loud banging on the front door.

"Sandra must have forgotten her key," Christine said, and rose from the table to let her friend in.

It was not the most auspicious of times for her friend to return. Christine was now intent on effecting a reconciliation between the two men and Sandra was bound to be unsympathetic towards the situation. She would have to understand that it was critical that she stay in her room and keep out of any argument with the Courtneys.

However, when Christine opened the front door, she was totally unprepared for what happened. She was almost flattened against the wall as Cynthia Courtney pushed past her. Howard was on her heels. Prudence and Trevor came next. The two psychiatrists followed, backed up by two brawny men in white coats. They all charged down the hallway without so much as a by your leave to the owner of the house.

"There he is!" Cynthia cried. "Completely out of his mind!"

Shane's voice rang out, hard and menacing. "Take one more step towards my grandfather and you get a broken head from me."

Christine pushed past the invaders to find Shane standing beside Max, his legs belligerently spread apart, the silver-tipped walking cane grasped threateningly in his hands.

Max tapped his arm. "Nothing to worry about, my boy. Everything foreseen and taken care of."

"What are you doing here, Shane?" Howard demanded. "You've got no business with the family any more. You were thrown out years ago."

"He's here because I want him here!" Christine declared, whirling in outrage on the pack of intruders. "What right have you got to come storming into my house?"

"She's the one!" Prudence pointed. "Fifty years younger than him!"

"Didn't think we'd find out where she lived, did you, Dad?" Trevor crowed triumphantly. "We've had this house watched for days. We knew you'd come to her sooner or later."

Good lord! Sandra was right, Christine thought, and felt outraged that she had been spied upon.

"Yes! The old goat was going to pay her five thousand dollars a week to hold his hand and take his temperature!" Cynthia screeched. "God only knows what would have developed from that!"

"Bribed the ward sister to get her address," Howard put in smugly. "You underestimated us, Dad."

"How much did you pay?" Max demanded.

"Five hundred dollars!"

"Couldn't negotiate your way out of a paper bag," Max said in disgust.

The ward sister was doing very well out of this, Christine thought, then swung into attack again. "You're completely out of line!" she accused the gang of four. "I didn't take the job."

"Little gold-digger!" sneered Cynthia.

"Watch your tongue, Aunt Cynthia!" Shane grated. "I will not have Christine insulted."

"Look! You and that nurse can do what you like, Shane. We've got to get Dad certified," Trevor said appeasingly.

"Yes. You're out of it anyway." Howard backed him up. "It doesn't affect you if he scatters the family fortune far and wide."

"The whole lot of you are more certifiable than my grandfather is," Shane retorted fiercely. "You get him locked up over my dead body!"

Max patted Shane's arm again. "You're a fine boy, Shane. Don't know why we ever disagreed." He reached into his coat pocket and pulled out a long envelope. "Pass that on to Howard. He's the eldest. That's if we excuse Cynthia for forging her birth certificate."

"What's this?" Howard demanded suspiciously.

"Photocopies of sworn statements, testifying to my soundness of mind. As of today," Max said with ringing satisfaction. "Apart from highly distinguished members of the medical profession, there's a chief justice of the high court, three ministers of the Crown, one ex-prime minister, and various other people of impeccable standing, all of whom are convinced that I have full possession of my faculties."

He smiled at the two psychiatrists and the men in the white coats. "Any argument from you gentlemen?"

Before they could answer there was a rallying yell of "Charge!" from outside and the sound of stampeding feet coming down the hallway. The two men in white coats got hammered against the wall, the psychiatrists did their best to shrink, and the gang of four were swept into a huddle at the other end of the living room by a bigger and more belligerent crowd of invaders.

Christine saw Shane raise the walking cane and screamed, "No! No, Shane! They're the regulars from Kitty O'Shea's."

Gino came steaming in, his arms raised in alarm. "Christine! Christine!" He could have rivalled Pavarotti in an operatic performance.

"I'm here, Gino!"

"Ah, my beautiful bambino!" He grabbed her arms and gave her a smacking kiss on both cheeks. "I keep my promise. We save you from these rapists and murderers."

Then in triumphal march came the leader of the band, big Mike Donovan, with Sandra Allsop perched on his shoulders as his guiding light.

She pointed to Shane. "He's the one who got Christine upstairs and took over her house!"

Then she swung her finger to Max. "And he's the one who paid me a thousand dollars to move out so I couldn't be a witness!"

The cavalry had arrived with a vengeance!

CHAPTER TWELVE

CHRISTINE CLOSED her eyes and took a deep breath. Why did everything have to happen all at once? She had been doing so well with Shane and Max before the Courtney entourage had descended upon them. Although, ironically enough, that had resulted in grandfather and grandson becoming a united front without any help from her at all.

Now this!

She heaved a sigh and opened her eyes to see big Mike lifting Sandra down from her perch and setting her safely on her feet. He tossed back his ponytail, expanded his huge barrel chest, which was barely clothed in a fringed leather bolero, then stepped into the centre of the room, his bristling beard defying anyone to shift him.

There was a chorus of approving growls. The men from Kitty O'Shea's had their blood up. Several of them formed a semicircle around Max and Shane, guarding the accused from any possible escape. The rest were keeping a threatening eye on the other captives, intimidating them into submission.

Mike took his time looking Shane up and down.

"Right, mate!" he challenged. "Have you got something to say before you get the treatment for fooling around with our girl?"

Christine had to stop this. "Mike—" she stepped forward, her arms outstretched, appealing to all of them "—it's all right."

"Christine," Shane cut in firmly, "I can answer for myself."

There were grunts of agreement around the room.

Christine was left with only one option. She went to stand beside Shane, thereby showing her allegiance.

"Blindly besotted," Sandra muttered, sadly shaking her head.

"Say your piece," Mike commanded, eyeing Shane with unshaken suspicion.

Shane swept his gaze around the room, fearlessly meeting the accusing eyes directed at him. "Firstly, I want to say that from the moment I chanced upon Christine, I felt she was the most unique and special person I've ever met. Your presence here tonight, so many loyal and true friends ready to protect her from any harm, regardless of possible danger to yourselves, shows me how very special and unique she is to you all."

He faced Mike directly. "I assured you that I would look after her, Mike. And to the best of my ability, I have."

He nodded to Sandra. "I know I frightened Christine's friend when she arrived unexpectedly. Both

Christine and I thought a burglar was in the house and I did what I did to protect her and her property."

"What about all the things *you've* been doing to Christine's house?" Sandra put in.

"Every one of them improvements. Extra comforts for her. At no cost to Christine," Shane replied. "I tried to help you as well, Sandra. Because you're her friend. There is nothing I would not do for Christine. As to fooling with her—"

Again he sent his gaze around the onlookers, meeting every eye. "I, also, would pummel any man who looked like bringing harm to her. I know how you feel. I respect the stand you're making for her sake. I'm deeply moved that Christine has friends who care so much for her and her welfare. I care, too. More than I can say."

He paused a moment. The mood of the room had subtly changed. Hostility had sunk into galvanised attention.

"It may seem to you all that I've moved too fast where Christine is concerned," Shane continued. "I can only tell you that is the urgency of my feeling for her." He slid an arm around her waist. "I want to hold her to me for the rest of my life. I've asked Christine to marry me. I think she wants to. I hope she wants to. And if I succeed in persuading her to say yes, I'd be proud and happy for you all to come to our wedding."

There were a few murmurs of approval at this declaration.

Shane tightened his hold on her. "Whatever Christine decides, I will still want to look after her. Always. Above all else, I want her to be happy."

The only sound in the room was Max Courtney using his handkerchief.

Mike cleared his throat and looked at Christine. "He sounds fairly genuine, Christine. Will we still give him the treatment?"

"Nothing has happened with Shane that I didn't want to have happen, Mike," she answered huskily.

Shane's long speech had brought a huge lump of emotion to her throat. The idea of him being ruthlessly self-interested simply could not be upheld anymore. Having her with him was his only purpose, and he had pursued it with a single-minded devotion that Christine could no longer doubt.

"Are you going to marry him, Christine?" Gino called out.

Before she could reply, the Courtney family snapped out of submission.

"Absolutely not!" Cynthia cried.

"Disgrace to the family!" Prudence sneered.

"You're still under investigation!" Trevor revealed threateningly.

"Entirely unsuitable!" Howard declared.

There was a rumble of discontent around the room. Christine quickly forestalled any action by disdaining to answer these contentious comments. She spoke directly to Gino.

"A woman has the right to decide for herself when and if she accepts a proposal of marriage. As you've just heard, there's some opposition from Shane's family that needs to be sorted out. But when I do make up my mind, Gino, Shane will be the first to know."

"Fair enough!" said Mike, then glared at the gang of four who had dared to register disapproval of a marriage he was beginning to favour. "Men, I reckon we'll be doing Christine good if we throw this lot out."

Besides drinking beer, throwing people out was the one activity the men from Kitty O'Shea's knew best how to do. They all brightened at the prospect. Hands flexed in anticipation.

"We'll go quietly," said Howard nervously.

"My oath, you will!" said Mike. "And not another peep out of you against our girl."

"Who'd want to stay amongst this rabble?" Prudence said most imprudently.

"Right!" said one of the men. "That big-mouthed dame is mine!"

There was a surge of gleefully aggressive humanity across the room.

"Take your hands off me," squawked Trevor. "I'll lay assault charges."

"Try that and we'll investigate you, mate! Teach you how it's done," one wit proclaimed, starting off a round of cheerfully ribald comments as the gang of four and their entourage were swept out in a wild melee. The last that was heard of them was Cynthia's shriek of outrage as they were forcefully helped into the street.

A stream of advice flowed after them.

"That's just a taste of what's coming if you try mucking up Christine and her man."

"Yeah! Be grateful you got off lightly this time."

"And keep your noses out of their private business."

"Or you'll have us to answer to!"

Mike led the mob to the living room, dusting off his hands with great aplomb. Everyone trooped in after him, their faces beaming with satisfaction in the justice of their cause and the pleasure of a job well done. Christine couldn't help feeling that the vultures had got their just desserts. She was smiling happily at her sturdy band of supporters when the next bombshell burst.

"You forgot about him," Sandra cried, pointing accusingly at Max.

"No!" cried Christine. "He's just recovering from a heart attack. I was nursing him at the hospital. And he had nothing to do with the watchers, Sandra. The people who were thrown out were responsible for that."

Sandra's face lit up with triumph. "Then I was right about the blue car and the grey car."

Christine nodded. "They had my house under surveillance."

Max rose to his feet, addressing Sandra in a booming voice. "Don't be worrying about me, young woman. I'm right behind the action you've taken. You did well to report what was going on to this fine body of men. You deserve a substantial reward."

"I do?" Sandra said in surprise.

"Of course, you do. Thanks to your initiative, I won't be needing your room tonight. The important thing's been settled with Shane and Christine, and now other action is called for. But keep the money, my dear. A gift of gratitude from me."

"You mean it?" Sandra squeaked incredulously.

"Not only do I mean it, but all these fine men deserve a reward as well. Best night's work I've seen in many a day," he said with relish. "The drinks are on me at Kitty O'Shea's."

There was a rousing cheer of approval.

"Hold it!" Mike commanded. "If you're buying us drinks, mate, you'd better tell us who you are."

"Call me Max." He clapped Shane on the shoulder. "I'm the grandfather of this fine boy. And my dearest wish is that Christine will decide to marry him. It'll be the making of him. And by God, I'll do my utmost to look after her, too. Best nurse in the hospital. Finest girl in the world. Is there any man here who can't drink to that?"

A clamour of voices assured him they could bend their elbows all night on that score. Mike threw an arm around Max's shoulders and scooped him along to lead the charge to Kitty O'Shea's.

"Max, you're not supposed to drink," Christine called out anxiously.

His triumphant voice floated over the press of men who followed him. "I'm not in hospital now, Sunshine!"

The last of them were disappearing out the front door when Max's head poked inside. Big Mike Donovan was hanging on to him like a limpet. They were obviously going to be soul mates. Sandra pushed past them, happily brandishing her fistful of dollars and obviously intent on celebrating with everyone else.

"Let that be a lesson to you, Shane," Max said with a huge grin. "I cleared the place for you and Christine." He gave them a big wink. "Age and experience will outwit youth and enthusiasm any day."

Christine felt Shane's chest expand, and she grabbed his arm hard. Only a sharp hiss escaped from his lips as he manfully bit down on the retort. The General gave them a jaunty salute and closed the door.

"Respect," Christine softly reminded Shane. "Your grandfather does deserve respect. Especially when he's right." She smiled, her eyes promising him a reward for his restraint under provocation. "We do have the house to ourselves."

Shane took another deep breath. His dark eyes burned at Christine. "I am going to lock and bolt the front door," he said with determination.

"I'm afraid it hasn't got a bolt, Shane," Christine said ruefully.

"I told you at the very beginning that I was a handyman. That door is going to be bolted tonight!"

Christine thought it was a waste of time and energy. She slid her hands up Shane's chest and moved closer to him. "I was very impressed by what you said to my friends, Shane."

Bolts were instantly driven out of his mind.

"Will you say yes now, Christine?" he asked, his arms winding around her to hold her pliant body firmly against his.

"Well, you could have been saying it all for effect. So you wouldn't get the treatment," she suggested archly, not believing that for a moment but wanting to bask in the wonderful certainty of his love for her.

"There's no way I'd be intimidated out of being with you," he defended hotly. "If they'd tried to separate us, they would have had the fight of their lives. Big Mike and all."

She glowed her admiration. "I was so proud of you, standing up to them with such manly resolve."

"I meant every word I said," he insisted fiercely.

"I must admit it sounded that way," Christine conceded, thrilled by the passionate throb in his voice.

"So?" His eyes glittered hopefully.

"You were only outbidding your grandfather when you first asked me to marry you," she reminded him, her bubbling inner joy demanding that every last cloud be dispelled from the future that was shining so brightly in her mind.

"Christine, right then I thought I had a problem about keeping you with me. The solution simply leapt off my tongue because it was what I wanted anyway. To have you with me always. I promise you that was the way it was."

"You didn't even ask me if it was what I wanted," Christine chided.

"I'm asking you now."

"You have a very arrogant way of assuming things, Shane Courtney."

"Isn't the feeling I have with you mutual, Christine?" he asked softly. "Can't I take that for granted?"

Impossible to deny what had been self-evident all week. And would be self-evident forever if its promise held true. "Marriage is a lifelong commitment for me, Shane."

"For me as well," he assured her. "Believe me, Christine, I want you beside me forever. I think even my grandfather has come to accept that as fact. Can't you?" he appealed.

"Why do you suppose he suddenly changed his mind about everything?"

"Saving face. When defeat is staring at you right down the gun barrel, a sidestep is in order," Shane said dryly.

"Well, I was proud of you for letting bygones be bygones and standing by him against your uncles and aunts."

Shane heaved an impatient sigh. "I would have stood by anybody against that lot," he growled. "Can we get to the important issue?"

"You're a very proud man."

"Even prouder with you at my side. Will you say yes?"

"I'm nearly at that point," she said encouragingly.

"What else do I need to do?" he asked.

She flicked open the top button of his shirt. "Perhaps if you remind me some more of our mutual feeling..."

"No problem," he said, and set about the task with an ardour that convinced Christine nothing could be more right than having Shane Courtney as her husband for the rest of her life.

It was just as well they had the house to themselves, because Shane's shirt got discarded in the hallway. Christine's bra was dropped off somewhere in the living room. By the time Shane started up the staircase, her nurse's uniform was bunched around her waist, only held up because her legs were wound around Shane's hips.

He had to feel for the treads with his feet because his eyes were closed, his entire concentration bent on worshipping Christine's breasts in a very erotic fashion. Her arms clung to his head, holding him with sweet possessiveness. It was a novel and exciting way of going upstairs, Christine thought. Everything about living with Shane was novel and exciting.

The picture formed in her mind of the life they could share together. That could be novel and exciting, too.

When she gave Shane her consent. Which would not be long now. After all, he was the most perfect upstairs lover in the whole world, and she knew the perfect moment was coming for her to say yes.

CHAPTER THIRTEEN

THE BEST OF EVERYTHING. It was what her mother had wanted for her. Yet as Christine's gaze wandered around the magnificent dining room in Max Courtney's country mansion, the grandeur of her surroundings did nothing to erase the underlying sadness of this first Christmas without her mother.

Of course she had Shane to give her a sense of belonging. And Max, who was already claiming her as his grand-daughter although the wedding was still a month away. She glanced at the emerald-and-diamond ring on her engagement finger, then smiled at Shane, wondering what the rest of the Courtney family was making of them being seated on either side of Max at the head of the table.

None of them had refused Max's invitation to join him for Christmas dinner. Howard and Cynthia's family sat on one side of the long table, Trevor and Prudence's on the other, all of them dressed to the nines and putting their best faces forward. They were steadfastly maintaining the position that nothing was amiss within the family. It was as though the raid on Christine's house at Paddington and the subsequent rout had never occurred.

It was probably the pragmatic choice to come and enjoy the best of everything while they could, Christine decided. And however much her presence might stick in their throats, they had been studiously polite to her. Max's home, and Max's wealth, and Max's approval, were strong incentives for good behaviour on a day that stood for peace and goodwill.

The war was over. Christine realised now it had never been a war for Shane. He did feel a bond with his grandfather, and had been willing to find a meeting ground with him if that was possible. Rather than lose his grandson again, Max had finally respected Shane's resolve to be his own man.

Christine remembered wondering six weeks ago how she would spend Christmas this year. She could never have envisaged such a place in a million years. This dining room alone was a shrine to wealth. The high cathedral ceiling, the French doors with the elegantly sashed drapes of rose silk sweeping into graceful pools on the polished wooden floor... Those were enough to take the breath away before one started to consider the furniture.

It was all gleaming cedar—the magnificent sideboard at the end of the room, cabinets filled with exquisite pieces of china and figurines, the table that could easily seat twenty people, the beautiful chairs upholstered in a silvery grey velvet into which had been woven a rose motive. The table itself had been set with an array of silverware and glassware fit for kings and queens. Max certainly did himself proud, Christine thought, and she began to appreciate how much it hurt his family to think of him giving it away.

To be accustomed to so much... She supposed life without it was unthinkable to the Courtneys. All except Shane, who had turned his back on it rather than accept compromising himself to his grandfather's will. Christine's heart swelled with love. Shane was above being bought with material things. It made her feel very secure with him. She knew that what he felt with her was more important to him than anything else.

Once the final course of the sumptuous dinner was cleared away, Max lifted his glass of champagne in a toast. "I wish you all a merry Christmas!" he said.

Everyone followed suit, and "Merry Christmas!" was echoed around the table.

"I have a private little gift ceremony to perform with my sons and their wives," Max announced. "Shane and Christine are also welcome to stay here with me. The Christmas tree awaits the rest of you in the lounge."

A quick exodus took place from the lower end of the table.

"Now comes the division of the spoils," Max declared.

There was a shudder of apprehension from the gang of four. Shane's air of nonchalance was in marked contrast. Christine was proud that it meant nothing to him, although she hoped his grandfather would give him something, no matter how small. A sign of peace between them.

Max lit a cigar, ignoring Christine's frown at his wilful defiance of good health practices. He smiled at her, then extended his smile to those tensely awaiting his pronouncements.

"Howard, Trevor, you are my sons. I know your strengths, your faults, your weaknesses. Because I love you, I've indulged you, giving you everything you've wanted. In all honesty I cannot blame you for the way you've chosen to live your lives. Much of the fault lies at my door."

He paused, took a puff of his cigar, then addressed them again. "I told you I was giving everything away. For the most part I have. But I cannot leave you unprovided for. Therefore, I'm giving each of you ten million shares in Courtney Enterprises. It's all that's left. Do with it what you will. It will either make you or break you. I hope you make the right choices, but from here on in, that's in your own hands."

Howard and Trevor sprang to their feet, rushing to pump their father's hand and clap his shoulder in an excess of relief and joy and gratitude. Cynthia and Prudence quickly joined them, gushing over him with affectionate hugs and kisses.

"We've always loved you, too, Dad," Howard said with an emotional catch in his voice.

"Best father a man could have," said Trevor, overcome with filial feeling.

"You know you can depend on us to do anything for you," Cynthia simpered.

"Just call on us. Any time," Prudence purred.

Christine saw Shane's lips curl into a sardonic little smile, and her heart twisted painfully at the preference given to those who had stayed to be yes-people to Max. She hoped Shane wouldn't be too hurt.

"Enough! Enough!" cried Max. "Go and join your families. I've given everything away. There's nothing left to interest you. I only have a few little bits and pieces to give to Shane and Christine."

They went willingly, exultation in their every step, and without so much as a sympathetic glance at the nephew who had been overlooked in favour of themselves.

"Well, Grandfather, you certainly made their day," Shane said without the slightest trace of acrimony. "I hope this makes yours."

He handed Max a small packet in Christmas wrapping. Max tore it apart as eagerly as a small boy with a surprise gift. No-one else had presented him with anything. He was delighted with the antique silver cigarcutter he finally uncovered.

"Shane! That's encouraging him," Christine chided in exasperation.

"No. It's accepting the inevitable," Shane dryly corrected her.

Max laughed at them both, then drew two envelopes from his pocket. "Now it's my turn," he said. He handed them both to Shane. "One for you, and one for your wife-to-be. You can give it to her on your wedding day."

Shane slit open one of the envelopes, withdrew a sheet of paper, scanned it quickly, then looked quizzically at his grandfather.

"There are only three of them. And I'm keeping one for sentimental reasons," Max said. "These shares are not even fully paid up."

"So what is each share worth, Grandfather?" Shane asked.

Max grinned. "Five cents."

Shane started to laugh. It was a joyous, wild belly laugh. "You're a real rogue, Grandfather! A villain!"

Max started to laugh, too, the two of them bellowing uproariously in mutual understanding and accord.

"What's so funny?" Christine pleaded.

"Three shares...at five cents each...control the might and wealth...of Courtney Enterprises... whatever's left of it," Shane gasped out between peals of laughter.

"Enough for you to make it work if you're as good as you think you are," Max challenged with merrily twinkling eyes.

"You're on, Grandfather. I'll make it work."

"I still don't understand," Christine pressed.

Max explained. "The two shares that you and Shane hold give you the power to decide what dividends will be paid to each class of shareholders. You can give yourselves as much or as little as you want. You can give the others as much or as little as you desire. Courtney Enterprises is effectively yours to do with as you will."

He shot Shane a sharp look of probing concern. "That's not to say you're to short-change the family. You're the strong one, Shane. I expect you to be big enough to carry them, no matter how badly they've short-changed you."

"I don't need to hit back at them, Grandfather," he said quietly, then gave Christine a smile that was luminous with love for her. "When you already have all you most want, it's easy to be generous."

Max nodded. "I thought it had to be that way."

Christine flushed with pleasure. "Please give both shares to Shane, Max. I don't deserve anything."

"No, Christine. We share everything equally," Shane insisted.

"I have a further reason," Max said, reaching over to take her hand. Suddenly there was a look of poignant sadness in his dark eyes. "The value of a gift is not in its worth. What I want to give you, Christine, is one of the least valuable of my possessions, yet the most treasured."

He drew from his pocket what looked like a fob watch and pressed it into her hand. It was old, and its silver casing was slightly dented. "Open it," he invited softly. "As I have done every night for twenty years."

It *was* a fob watch. But framed in the lid was a photograph. Christine stared at it in dazed wonder. The woman in the photograph was unmistakably her mother. She looked questioningly at Max.

"How did you get this? Where did it come from?"

"Your mother gave it me. She bought the watch for me at the Paddington Bazaar. I took the photograph of her that day. It was a good day."

"You knew my mother?"

Shane made a sound of startled understanding. He sat bolt upright, his whole body tensely concentrated on his grandfather's next words.

"She was the finest woman I ever knew. She lived by her own standards and values. Without compromise. She gave freely of herself to others with her wit and good humour. She imparted a sense of caring that recognised need and soothed hurt. She knew what she was, where she was going to, what she stood for, and she never deviated from her own inner truth."

Tears swam into Christine's eyes. "Yes," she whispered huskily. "That's how she was."

"I courted your mother."

"When was that?" Christine asked.

"You were only a toddler. Sometimes I took you for walks while your mother was working. Bought you ice-cream."

"You did? I remember that...but not who took me."

"It was me," Max said simply. "I wanted to give something. In all the time I pursued your mother, she would never take anything from me."

"What happened between you?"

"I pressed the issue. I thought then—and I still think—your mother was genuinely fond of me. I asked her to marry me."

"What did she say?" Christine asked softly, seeing the shadow of hurt in his eyes.

"She said the same things her daughter said to me some weeks ago. That my wealth had been the ruination of me." He gave a bittersweet smile. "I've finally done what she told me to do. Given it all away. I'm sorry I couldn't do it when it counted."

He shook his head regretfully. "I couldn't keep seeing Rose after that. It tore me in two, Christine. I never saw her again. But I went to her funeral. You were heavily veiled. You wouldn't have seen me there. I stood alone in the background, thinking of all I'd missed and wishing it could have been different."

Shane leaned forward, understanding dawning on his face. "So that's why..."

"Yes. I didn't realise that my Sunshine was Rose's daughter until you came to the hospital and told me her background. Then I thought..."

"I would never have used that to spite you in any way, Grandfather," Shane said in pained protest. "Even if I'd known. Which I didn't. I swear to you."

Max patted his hand. "I realise that now. It was the shock, my boy. When you started talking about Kitty O'Shea's Hotel, it brought it all back. Something very private to me. Very special. And it hurt. I couldn't believe in the coincidence. It seemed more likely to me that you'd identified the photograph you'd seen in my watch."

Shane shook his head. "I saw, but it didn't connect in my mind. Not until now."

Max nodded. "I'm sorry I misread the situation so badly, Shane. Misjudged you..."

"If I hadn't been so hot-headed—"

"Chip off the old block."

They looked ruefully at each other, acknowledging the likeness that would always be a bond between them.

Then Max turned to Christine. "I loved your mother. She was the only woman I ever truly loved. I couldn't let my grandson use her daughter, hurt you, but it was so obvious that you were smitten with him."

"It was more than that, Max," Christine said quietly.

"Strange how the wheel turns," he mused. "My grandson falling in love with Rose Delaney's daughter." He smiled at Shane. "When you said how you felt about Christine to the men from Kitty O'Shea's, that was how it was with me when I first met Rose. She was utterly unique. Special. She stood apart from all others."

Christine pressed his hand. "Thank you for telling me. And for this gift. I'll treasure it, too, Max. I miss my mother, and this, my first Christmas without her..."

"Rose is here, Christine," he said softly. "She's here in you, my dear. And, please God, she will be in my great-grandchildren. And they will play in this house, and sit under the Christmas tree, and all I have now will be theirs."

Christine's eyes widened. "You don't mean..."

"I could not think of a more worthy cause. And to know part of my Rose will live on in my family, being able to enjoy all I wanted to lay at her feet, that makes my life worthwhile."

Max pushed his chair back, rose to his feet and clapped Shane on the shoulder. "This boy takes after me, you know. No-one better to be head of the family. And you, my dear Sunshine, will keep his feet on the straight and narrow."

She rose from the table and gave him a deeply emotional hug. Words were impossible. Max cleared his throat and said gruffly, "Enough is enough. Life must go on. I've got things to do."

"Like what?" said Shane suspiciously.

"I'm taking Sandra Allsop off to Tahiti this evening. She likes Gauguin's paintings and she's never been there. I'll have some bright young company to amuse me, and you'll have all the privacy you want in your house. We'll be back in time for the wedding."

Christine drew away from him in alarm. "What about your heart?"

"I'm taking the ward sister along with us. Great negotiator, that woman. I couldn't resist having her as my private nurse."

He manoeuvred Christine into Shane's ready embrace. "Merry Christmas! Merry Christmas! And a merry Christmas to me, too!"

Then he was off to join the rest of the family, leaving Shane and Christine to follow when they wanted to.

"We are going to have to look after your grandfather, Shane," Christine said purposefully.

"Rainy day," was Shane's enigmatic and amused reply.

"What's that supposed to mean?" she asked.

He grinned, his dark eyes dancing sheer unholy devilment. "If Grandfather hasn't salted a couple of million away for a rainy day, I'll eat my hat."

Christine looked down at the old silver fob watch in her hand. The catch was worn and the two halves didn't quite fit precisely together anymore. There was no doubt in her mind that Max had opened it every night for twenty years.

"That's why the photograph of your mother was familiar to me," Shane said softly. "I saw it in there quite accidentally many years ago. My grandfather dropped the watch. It fell open. I picked it up for him. I remember now that he wouldn't answer my questions about the woman. He got angry with me for asking."

"He's a wonderful man," Christine murmured, then looked at Shane with a slightly wobbly smile.

"I won't argue with that." Shane returned her smile. "I always thought he was."

His arms tightened around her. "But you're even more wonderful," he murmured, and proceeded to kiss his bride-to-be almost senseless.

When she finally came up for breath, Christine asked, "How do you think the family will take this, Shane?"

His mouth twisted. "They won't care as long as the money keeps rolling in."

"And this house?"

"I guess this house is the meeting ground, Christine."

"Yes. Yes, it is." In every way, Christine thought.

"How does a long line of Christmases here sound to you?"

She smiled. "Peace and goodwill."

"And love."

"Always love," she agreed.

"I adore you. And the more I know you, the more I adore you."

"You say the loveliest things, Shane."

Then they kissed some more to make sure they had everything perfectly right.

CHAPTER FOURTEEN

THE HANDS OF THE CLOCK in the Paddington town hall tower pointed to the sixth hour. The grounds around the church and school were packed with people. It was as though the bazaar had not ended two hours earlier. Late-afternoon sunshine dappled through the plane trees, which were festooned with white ribbons. Musicians played in the street. A festive air pervaded the whole scene as the colourful crowd gave expression to their pleasure in the occasion.

The limousine slowly pulled to a halt directly in line with the huge tubs of flowers that formed an avenue to the front door of the church. The chauffeur did his maestro act, and Gino emerged onto the pavement, his roly-poly body resplendent in white tie and tails. He raised his arms to the crowd.

"The bride!" he announced with all his Italian sense of theatre and romance.

The cheers were loud enough to bring all Paddington to a halt as Christine stepped out of the limousine to acknowledge her well-wishers. There were oohs! and aahs! of delighted admiration as the full glory of her bridal dress with its long train and even longer veil billowed out behind her.

Gino proudly wound her arm around his. "You look like a princess," he said, his eyes filling with emotional tears. "I wish your mamma were here to see you. She would be so happy."

And Christine knew in her heart that it was Rose's daughter everyone had come to see. They had gathered to wish her all the happiness her mother would have wished her. Rose Delaney had touched all their lives with something special.

She moved forward, accepting what her mother's friends had come to give, reaching out to them, returning their greetings, posing for their photographs for memories they held dear, smiling as her mother had once smiled. Sunshine through tears.

Then it was time to move into the church. The organ boomed out the wedding march, and Gino slowly and majestically escorted her down the aisle to give her away to the man whose life would be forever after joined to hers.

On the left of the aisle were all her mother's closest friends. On the right were the Courtney family and all their closest friends. Two vastly different worlds, Christine thought. Yet rich or poor, they were all people, subject to the feelings that coursed through humanity everywhere. Only the circumstances that shaped their lives were different. Too little...too much...

Her mother had recognised that, seeing through Max's wealth to the emptiness of his inner life. Max himself had finally seen what he had done to his children, and forgiven them their fears and inadequacies. The principle was not to judge others on what they showed, but to look into their hearts and seek understanding for what they did.

Shane turned to watch her come to him. Christine smiled, her face radiant with love for everyone. But especially for Shane. Their life together would be novel and exciting, but they would never let power or wealth distort what was truly important. The sharing and the caring...the inner truth her mother had implanted and nurtured with her own life.

Shane had told her it was sharing her world with him, showing him the caring, that had made him so ruthlessly determined to do anything, break down any walls in his way, anything to be with her for the rest of his life, to come in from the cold of the loneliness he had lived with for so long before they met, before he felt the heart-warming magic of how life could be with her.

I'll keep you warm, she promised him, as he held out his hand to her. You'll never be alone again, my love.

Their fingers touched and Gino reverently stood aside for Christine to join her husband-to-be.

The marriage ceremony began.

It was a simple service, yet every word felt intensely meaningful. Christine knew Shane felt it, too. It was in his voice, in his touch, in his eyes, as he made his vows to her, as he listened to her make the same vows to him. When they kissed as man and wife, it was as though a current of love flowed between them, bonding them for all time.

They moved to the altar to sign the register and the marriage certificate, and at the back of the church guitars were strummed. Big Mike Donovan lifted his voice into a slow and sentimental rendition of Christine's song. "When Irish eyes are smiling..."

It seemed to Christine that every face in the church was smiling at her and Shane as they completed the signing and were handed the certificate. It was such a happy song, a song to lift any heart into feeling good. And that, Christine decided, was the true essence of *the best of everything*...what her mother had wanted for her. Simply feeling good.

When the old Irish folk song ended, the organ took over with its more formal music. Christine had never felt better in her whole life as she exultantly linked arms with Shane and they swept down the aisle, the new Mr. and Mrs. Courtney.

Outside the church they were showered with rice and confetti, and happily submitted themselves to a barrage of photographs. The traffic on Oxford Street was stopped as people poured across the road to Kitty O'Shea's. They formed a guard of honour for the bride and groom, ensuring them a stately passage to the hotel.

There was much revelry in Kitty O'Shea's that night, and many an old song was sung. But the one that meant the most was kept to the end. As the bride and groom were taking their leave of all the guests, the band started up once more and Mike Donovan poured his heart and soul into the dear familiar words.

My wild Irish Rose...

There was a huge upswell of deeply emotional sound as voices from both floors of the hotel joined in.

The sweetest flower that grows
You may search everywhere
But none can compare
With my wild Irish Rose.

There were tears in Max Courtney's eyes as he hugged his new grand-daughter-in-law goodbye. Shane swept her away to the waiting limousine.

"Where are we going?" she asked him as they drove off into the night.

Shane smiled his perfect smile, his dark eyes adoring her. "To the end of the road," he said. "Wherever it may lead. Together. Forever."

It was a sentiment close to Christine's heart. She smiled at her husband, her partner, her lover. Together. Forever.

AUTHOR'S NOTE

Kitty O'Shea's is a real hotel. It is situated as described in this story, across from the church and school grounds where the Paddington Bazaar is held every Saturday. The restaurant in the hotel is described as it was seen by the author. On her visit, one Sunday afternoon, a band played Irish songs.

Her husband was going into St. Vincent's Hospital that afternoon, and it was extremely doubtful whether he would ever come out. We outlined much of the story at that lunch, and it was decided that this book would not reflect how we truly felt at the time, but would be full of love and laughter and the joy of life. We hope we succeeded.

The depiction of the men from Kitty O'Shea's is completely fictitious. None of these people are personally known to the author, and the actions given to them in this book were given for dramatic purposes only. The hotel employees in this story are fictitious, as is the working background of Rose Delaney. The cul-de-sac where Christine has her home is entirely imaginary.

HARLEQUIN ◆ PRESENTS®

A Year
DOWN UNDER

In 1993, Harlequin Presents celebrates the land down
under. In June, let us take you to the Australian Outback,
in OUTBACK MAN by Miranda Lee,
Harlequin Presents #1562.

Surviving a plane crash in the Australian Outback is
surely enough trauma to endure. So why does Adrianna
have to be rescued by Bryce McLean, a man so gorgeous
that he turns all her cherished beliefs upside-down? But
the desert proves to be an intimate and seductive setting
and suddenly Adrianna's only realities are the red-hot
dust *and* Bryce....

Share the adventure—and the romance—
of A Year Down Under!

Available this month in
A YEAR DOWN UNDER

SECRET ADMIRER
by Susan Napier
Harlequin Presents #1554
Wherever Harlequin books are sold.

Take 4 bestselling love stories FREE

Plus get a FREE surprise gift!

Special Limited-time Offer

Mail to Harlequin Reader Service®

3010 Walden Avenue
P.O. Box 1867
Buffalo, N.Y. 14269-1867

YES! Please send me 4 free Harlequin Presents® novels and my free surprise gift. Then send me 6 brand-new novels every month, which I will receive months before they appear in bookstores. Bill me at the low price of $2.24 each plus 25¢ delivery and applicable sales tax, if any. * I understand that accepting the books and gift places me under no obligation ever to buy any books. I can always return a shipment and cancel at any time. Even if I never buy another book from Harlequin, the 4 free books and the surprise gift are mine to keep forever.

106 BPA AJCG

Name	(PLEASE PRINT)	
Address		Apt. No.
City	State	Zip